JEN CALONITA

DISNEP • HYPERION

Los Angeles   New York

First Edition, September 2021
10 9 8 7 6 5 4 3 2 1
FAC-020093-21218
Printed in the United States of America

This book is set in Agmena Pro/Linotype
Designed by Phil T. Buchanan

Library of Congress Cataloging-in-Publication Data
Names: Calonita, Jen, author.
Title: The rise of Flynn Rider / by Jen Calonita.
Other titles: Tangled (Motion picture)
Description: First edition. • Los Angeles : Disney Hyperion, 2021. •
   Series: [Lost legends ; vol 1] • Audience: Ages 8-12. • Audience: Grades
   7-9. • Summary: "Tangled's Eugene Fitzherbert goes on a life-altering
   adventure that leads to his transformation into the one and only Flynn
   Rider" — Provided by publisher.
Identifiers: LCCN 2020052116 • ISBN 9781368044868 (hardcover) • ISBN
   9781368050852 (ebook)
Classification: LCC PZ7.C1364 Ris 2021 • DDC [Fic] — dc23
LC record available at https://lccn.loc.gov/2020052116

Reinforced binding
Visit www.DisneyBooks.com

For Chris Sonnenburg, who braved the Long Island Rail Road and Uber during rush hour to talk all things Eugene Fitzherbert with me

PROLOGUE
12 YEARS AGO . . .

King Edmund was not a rash man.

That's why he'd spent the last nine months hatching the perfect plan. The idea began to grow like a persistent itch the moment his wife announced she was pregnant. It didn't matter if he was sitting in a council meeting, reading former kings' writings in the library, or quietly walking the castle halls — the king had become a man obsessed. The servants noticed. So did his wife.

"Edmund?" she whispered, shaking him awake late one night.

"What?" Edmund sat up with a start, his heart pounding.

"You were yelling in your sleep again."

He grabbed a handkerchief and wiped the perspiration from his forehead. It took him a moment to realize where he was, but when he looked over and saw the terrified look in his wife's beautiful brown eyes, he attempted a calm smile. "Oh, darling, I'm sorry I woke you. I'm fine."

"Are you sure?" she asked worriedly. "You were tossing and turning and mumbling something."

Moonlight was seeping through the window. Edmund prayed his wife wouldn't be able to read his expression. "Oh? What was it?" "'Destroy the stone,'" she said, her voice higher than normal. The two of them looked at one another for a moment. "Edmund, you aren't . . ."

"It's nothing for you to worry about." He patted her hand reassuringly. "It was just a nightmare. Go back to sleep."

But it wasn't a nightmare. Destroying the Moonstone Opal had become King Edmund's mission. For centuries before him, kings in the Dark Kingdom had been tasked with protecting the powerful stone created when a single drop of moonlight fell to the earth. Now that duty had fallen to Edmund. He refused to allow his unborn child to someday suffer the same fate.

Being "protector" of the Moonstone Opal had never felt like the gift his own father made it out to be. The job was a curse. The kings before him had watched over the stone out of duty, not pride. How did you protect something that was continually trying to destroy the very air you breathed? That was slowly destroying the world around you with unbreakable black rocks that twisted and curved through every surface they touched? The Opal's defenses had only grown over time, creating thickets of vines and rocks that blocked out the rest of the world and eventually formed the very stone on which the Dark Kingdom now stood. This was the reason the gem was kept hidden in a vault below the castle's surface.

Sometimes Edmund swore he *felt* the Opal pulsing as if it were plotting its next move. Edmund knew the stories, passed down from father to son and king to king, about the death and destruction one tiny drop of moonlight had caused when it was left exposed, but he refused to be held prisoner by it anymore. He wanted the Moonstone Opal destroyed, even if it took him along with it.

Edmund didn't tell his wife he was thinking any of this, however. That was his first mistake.

Maybe if he had confessed, she would have helped him see reason. Then, on the night their child was born, when he was holding his son in his arms and his wife had asked, "What are you thinking about?" Edmund could have said, "I'm thinking about destroying the Moonstone so our son's destiny will be different from my own."

He didn't, but his wife somehow knew the truth, as wives usually do. His beautiful wife, with her charming smile and biting wit, had always been much smarter than he was. (Forgetting that had been his second mistake.)

Two weeks after the birth of their son, she secretly followed him down to the underground vault where the Moonstone was kept. He didn't notice her crossing the long bridge behind him that led to the cage where they kept the Opal hostage. And he didn't see her hiding behind a pillar on the bridge, watching as he made his third mistake — opening the cage and exposing the Opal to the world.

As he had practiced in his head so many times before, Edmund lifted the poison-laced hatchet above his head and prepared to smash the Opal with it. "May this place and the cursed power that lies within it be forever wiped from existence!" he shouted.

Instead of breaking the Opal, the hatchet froze millimeters above it. Angered, the Moonstone began to glow and pulse. Before Edmund could react, the hatchet shattered into a million pieces.

Several pieces pierced Edmund's shoulder, and he fell to the ground as the chamber began to quake. Spiky black rocks broke through the walls, rumbling so fiercely they sounded like voices. *You fool!* they seemed to shout. *You think a dagger could destroy us? You will pay dearly, King!*

And pay dearly Edmund did, as a black spike shot straight through the floor and pierced his right arm. Edmund cried out as he yanked his arm free and forced himself to rise.

I must warn the others! Edmund thought as he staggered back toward the bridge. *I must save my family!* He could picture his son sleeping peacefully alongside his wife in their chambers high above the vault. He had to reach them!

"Edmund!"

He turned around, and immediately his heart gave a lurch. His wife was standing in the center of the bridge in her nightdress, her brown hair spilling around her shoulders as the walls started to come down around her. Fear was written all over her beautiful face.

Edmund staggered toward the bridge to reach her. *I'm sorry! I was a fool,* he wanted to shout. *Forgive me.* But the bridge gave way before he had the chance.

Edmund watched in horror as his beloved wife plummeted into the dark recesses of the cavern below. In shock, he collapsed against the wall next to him. *Let death come,* he thought, as the walls continued to shake. But then he remembered.

The baby.

He had to get to him! Invigorated, Edmund frantically looked around for an escape. The bridge was gone and he was trapped on the same side of the vault as the angered Moonstone. But then the wall behind him began to crumble, making an opening to what appeared to be the sewers. Could they lead to a way out?

Edmund had to try. Step by step, he dragged himself toward the tunnel, climbing through the hole and following a stream of water until he spotted stairs. Relieved, he climbed them and pushed his way through a rusty trapdoor.

But his relief only lasted a second. He realized the situation in the castle was as bleak as it had been below. Black rocks had pushed their way into the fortress, taking down walls and frightening his subjects, who were running in every direction, looking for a way out of the madness. Maeve, his wife's most trusted handmaiden, spotted him climbing out of the ground.

"My king!" Maeve helped him up. "The Opal's powers have been unleashed!"

I caused this and I will never forgive myself, he wanted to tell her, but all he could think about was his wife's face as the bridge gave way. He let out a choked sob.

Maeve ripped off her white apron and used it as a tourniquet for his injured arm. "We have to get you somewhere safe," she said and began to help him down the hall.

"The boy?" Edmund asked urgently. "Where is he now? Is he all right?"

"Yes, my king," Maeve said, and Edmund heard himself exhale. "When the destruction started, I ran to your chambers. I couldn't find you or the queen, so I took the baby and put him in the care of the other serving girls till I could find you." She looked around. "Where is the queen, sire?"

All around them, rocks were laying waste to their beautiful castle, destroying their home. But Edmund's true home had already perished because of his carelessness.

His voice was barely a whisper. "Gone."

Maeve covered her mouth in shock.

They both jumped as part of the central staircase collapsed as a long black rock sped straight through the foyer. Servants and subjects ran for cover, hoping to find somewhere safe to hide. Edmund knew all too well there wasn't anywhere to go.

Instead of trying to destroy the Opal, he should have found a way to contain the Moonstone. Maybe that was his true fate, he realized.

THE RISE OF FLYNN RIDER

If he stayed here and finished the job, his son might have a fighting chance.

"You must tell everyone to leave," Edmund said suddenly, and Maeve's eyes widened. "It's no longer safe to stay in the Dark Kingdom. I want you all to go to the cable-car station immediately. The cars will get you to safety."

The cable cars were the only way on or off the fortress where their kingdom stood. With any luck, the rocks wouldn't have destroyed the station yet. Another rock sliced through the castle floor, making the ground shake.

"Go! Now!" he boomed, pushing Maeve away. "There isn't much time. I will stay here to make sure you've all made it out safely."

"But, my king . . ." Maeve began to protest.

Edmund already knew what she was thinking. He clasped her hand. "You will take the boy with you." His voice softened. "Find him somewhere safe, Maeve." He swallowed hard. "He cannot stay here."

"But, sire!" Maeve tried again.

Edmund cut her off. The pain from his arm was nothing compared to what he was feeling in his heart. "Please, Maeve, he can never know the truth about who he really is. I don't want him to come back here and suffer the same fate as me." He swallowed hard. "It is my duty to contain the Moonstone, not his."

Both the king's and Maeve's eyes began to well as they stared at each other, feeling the weight of what he was asking. But before either could say something that might change the other's mind, a black rock shot up through the floor, separating them.

"Go! Get the boy!" Edmund cried.

Maeve hesitated once more. "But, my king, please! You must come with us!"

Edmund smiled sadly. "We both know I cannot. If I do not stay behind to stop it, there will be nowhere left for either of you to go. *Please.* His mother would want me to give him a fighting chance." Glass shattered as a rock pierced a window by Edmund's head. "Now go! No one stays behind but me! That's an order."

"Yes, sire," she said tearfully before turning to the others and repeating what the king had told her. The news spread like wildfire, and people began moving in great waves to the castle doors, where cable cars would hopefully still be waiting.

Edmund was too overwhelmed to address his people. His wife was gone. His kingdom destroyed. His plan hadn't been strong, but all was not lost. He would stay here and fight this monstrous gem until he could find a way to destroy it once and for all. And when that day finally came, he swore on his wife's life, he would make things up to their son.

"King Edmund?"

When he looked up, he saw Maeve holding a small bundle in her arms.

Somehow through all the chaos, the boy was still sleeping. The king watched his small pink face dreaming and felt a mix of pride and anguish. Maeve tried to give the boy to him, but Edmund put up his hand to stop her. Instead, he rested his fingers on the baby's chest, feeling his little heart beating. It sounded strong. That was good. He would need strength to make it out there in the world alone. Something told him that with his mother's charm and wit and his own bravado, this child would find his way.

"The last cable car is here!" someone shouted, and Edmund motioned for Maeve to go.

"Your Highness, please," she begged, but Edmund shook his head.

He had important things to tell her and very limited time. "Remember: I don't want you to tell him anything about this horrible place or the life he left behind." Edmund felt a lump begin to form in his throat. He swallowed hard. "Staying away is his best chance. Promise me you will honor my word."

"I promise," Maeve said as she fought back tears.

Edmund nodded. He wished there were something more he could give the child, but there was no time. He looked around at the crumbling room, and his eyes landed on the bookshelf. "Wait!" he said, dragging himself over to it. He gathered a stack of books, dropped them into a sack lying on the floor, and then handed it to Maeve. "See to it that these stories stay with him. I always thought we'd read these together someday, but now . . . at least he will still have them."

She took the bag and smiled. "He will like that, sire. Thank you."

Edmund swallowed hard again and looked at the boy one last time. He bent down, and his lips grazed the child's forehead. The boy stirred. "May life treat you well, my son," he whispered. "Someday I hope we will meet again."

⊙NE

"IF MAKING FRIENDS WITH A TRUSTY STEED WERE EASY,
EVERYONE WOULD HAVE A RIDE."

—FLYNNIGAN RIDER IN *FLYNNIGAN RIDER AND THE RIDE TO THE RIVER'S EDGE*

"And that's all he wrote! Lights out, everyone!" Twelve-year-old Eugene Fitzherbert closed the book he was reading from with a loud clap. He was immediately met with a chorus of boos.

"You didn't finish the book!" shouted Leif.

Eugene maintained an air of innocence. "What do you mean?"

"You skipped the ending!" yelled Filip from the back of the room, where he was doing handstands.

"He hasn't even gotten to the stables yet!" agreed Rolf. "After he's caught in the stables there's a whole sword fight on horseback and then the big jump off the waterfall."

"We have to hear the sword fight!" moaned Leif. "That's the best part of the story."

"I don't know, fellas," Eugene said, secretly enjoying their outrage. "I'm pretty tired."

Was it so wrong to make the other kids prove they were paying attention? Read-alouds took a lot of time and effort.

Ha! Who was he kidding? He thrived on attention. Plus, he loved any chance to share his prized collection of Flynnigan Rider books.

Every night, before climbing into bed under thin quilts laid over even thinner mattresses, the lads at Miss Clare's Home for Boys would nestle around the fire and listen to Eugene read. The books were the only possessions he'd arrived at the orphanage with when he was a baby and he treated them like treasure. Every time he cracked open the frayed leather spine of one of the stories and breathed in the musty gold-leafed pages, it reminded him of *something*. He wasn't sure what exactly, but his gut feeling was his parents had read these stories to him once upon a time.

For that reason, he rarely let anyone touch the books, but he was always happy to share the stories aloud. And it had recently occurred to Eugene — just this night, in fact, at dinner, actually — why just read a book when you can act out a whole adventure?

However, if the boys wanted the full Eugene Fitzherbert experience, they'd need to work for it.

Leif fell to Flynn's feet and proceeded to beg. "Please finish the book! Pul-eeze?"

"I don't know . . ." Eugene hedged.

The other boys joined in on the begging.

Eugene was the one holding the power, and he couldn't help liking the feeling. Then he felt a tug on his patched pant leg.

"Please, Eugene?" said Marius in that tiny voice of his as he looked up at Eugene with big brown eyes. "I love this story."

Awww . . . Eugene rubbed Marius's brown hair before picking him up and placing him on a chair near the fire so he'd have a good seat for the action. "For you, anything."

"Yes!" Marius's fist pumped the air, and the other boys cheered and sat down again to listen.

He was a sucker for Marius. For all the younger boys, really. They were like one big family at the orphanage. Eugene couldn't complain. He had a roof over his head, food in his belly, and lots of boys ranging in age from three to twelve to hang out with. And they all loved Eugene's Flynn Rider books. How could they not? Flynn was a swashbuckling rogue, a charming friend to all, and the richest man alive. That meant he had enough money to go anywhere and do anything he wanted. For a kid with nothing, he was a pretty decent role model.

"But I'm getting a little tired of just reading, so we're going to mix things up a bit," Eugene said.

"What do you mean?" Rolf called out.

"I'm going to give you the full-blown Rider experience tonight," Eugene said with a smile. "But I'm going to need some help here."

Eugene surveyed the room, and half a dozen hands shot into the air. There was only one person he knew could help him with this. He turned to a short, dark-skinned boy who had been sitting on the window ledge quietly writing in his journal. "What do you say, Arnie? Want to help me pull off a one-of-a-kind reading tonight?"

Arnie raised his right eyebrow inquisitively at his friend. "I don't know. I'm kind of tired."

There were more groans from the boys.

"Come on, Arnie!" Leif grumbled. "You know Eugene will do a good job if you help him."

"We do make a good team," Eugene commented.

Arnie scratched his black hair, which was cut short, just the way he liked it. "That is true. Okay, I'm in." The other kids cheered even louder.

Perfect, Eugene thought. *Just as we planned at dinner.*

Everyone knew Arnwaldo Schnitz and Eugene Fitzherbert were as thick as thieves. Sure, they were different. While Eugene was chatty,

Arnie quietly observed. Eugene was obsessed with grooming (his hair was a constant battle), while Arnie focused on clothes. Eugene was fixated on someday finding his parents, while Arnie felt at home with the family he'd created with the boys in the orphanage. (Eugene joked Arnie might someday run the place.) And while Eugene loved to read, Arnie would rather spend his time jotting down notes in a small journal. But they were as close to brothers as two orphans could be.

Eugene and Arnie looked at each other, then got right to work.

"All right, fellas, we're going to give you a special reading tonight," Arnie declared. "But it requires everyone to clear the center of the room." He began to move chairs out of the way.

Eugene carefully placed the book on the sole bookshelf they had in the room (it only had three books on it). Then he rubbed his hands together and looked at the others. "So where were we? The stables!" He jumped up on a crate they used as a chair, and the boys started to cheer. "So there Flynn Rider was, tied to a fence post to be collected by Dr. Deserio's men in the morning. That thug had arrested Rider on bogus charges so he could steal his riches. He had no weapon to untie himself with, he'd lost his trusty pocketknife, and Dr. Deserio had stolen his horse. But was Flynn Rider ready to give up?"

"No!" the boys shouted, clearly delighted.

Feeding off their energy, Eugene jumped down and tiptoed across the room. "Flynn was smarter than Dr. Deserio! He waited for Dr. Deserio's guards to fall asleep, as guards inevitably do when they're overworked, slipped out of his restraints, and then he snuck over to the stables under the cover of darkness."

Eugene slipped into the shadows of the large room and approached the ladder that led up to the room's large loft, where many of the boys slept. "But did he use a door to enter the stables?"

"No!" chorused the boys.

"No! He climbed to the roof and entered through a hatch he had noticed earlier in the stable ceiling." Eugene reached the loft and stood up. "But before he dropped down to his horse so he could ride away, he watched to make sure no one was in the stable waiting for him. That's when he made his move."

This was his favorite part of the story, and their sleeping quarters were perfect for acting this part out. He reached up and tapped one of the rafter beams with his fist. A hidden compartment opened, revealing a rope that unfurled to the first floor. Eugene grabbed on to it and kicked off, swinging over the room. The boys whooped again and several ran to other hidden doors and compartments in the room, which revealed more ropes and pulleys and even a hidden gangplank that fell from a door in the loft and landed perfectly between two rafters.

"Rider hovered above the horses for a moment till he could see for certain the coast was clear, then he shimmied down again." Eugene climbed down and reached the ground. "Slowly, he made his way to his trusty steed, Oliver." Eugene approached Leif, who started to giggle uncontrollably, and petted the boy's head as if he were Flynn's horse. "It's okay, Oliver! I'm here to rescue you." He and Leif started walking across the room in tandem. "Rider climbed onto Oliver and slowly headed to the stable doors, sure he would be on his way to a new kingdom in no time."

"Not so fast, Rider!"

Eugene turned around. Arnie was standing on the wood plank high above him. He pointed a wooden sword at his friend. "That horse doesn't belong to you."

"Are you sure? I could have sworn I had a horse an hour ago, and I'm riding one now, so . . ." Eugene flashed a charming smile. "Finders keepers, Dr. Deserio." He tapped Leif's shoulder, and the two took off at a run across the room. Boys now hanging from pulleys and ropes swung out of the way as Arnie grabbed a rope and swung himself down to the floor.

"You're not going anywhere, Rider!" Arnie bellowed as he moved toward Eugene. "This barn is surrounded. You bust through those doors and you and your horse will be finished before you even can begin to gallop. Just give up already."

Eugene scratched his chin. "Giving up has never really been my style, Dr. Deserio. I thought you knew that by now." Eugene produced a sword from behind his back. Arnie did the same. The other boys started to whoop as the two began to battle their way across the room. Finally, Arnie backed Eugene into a corner.

Arnie pressed the sword to Eugene's chest. "Surrender, Rider!"

Eugene jumped up onto the large window seat to get away. "Me? Never!" Arnie climbed up after him.

"Watch the window!" Marius shouted.

But Eugene and Arnie weren't listening. Arnie swiped at Eugene's shoulder, and he pretended to stagger. Then Eugene swiped at Arnie's stomach, and his friend gave an "Oof!" Eugene jumped back down and began tying a rope around Leif's waist.

Arnie laughed. "What do you think you're going to do? Lift your horse in the air? It can't be done."

Eugene raised his eyebrows knowingly. "I've never been fond of the word 'can't.'" He tapped the floor, and the pulley holding Leif shot into the air. Eugene grabbed a second rope and followed while Arnie yelled and moaned at his loss. Eugene looked down at the boys watching. "Rider did lift Oliver into the air, even if he probably shouldn't have, because who lifts a horse? But Rider liked challenges, and taking Oliver back from Dr. Deserio was a challenge he wasn't going to lose."

"Guards!" Arnie shouted. "He's getting away!"

"Rider calculated the risks — jump with Oliver back to the first level and plow through the guards, or go higher, to the roof?" Eugene told the boys as he took a few steps back. "He and Oliver got into position and then took off at a run, preparing to create a Rider-and-Oliver-size hole in the roof, jump into a waiting carriage, and ride off into the night as Dr. Deserio stewed, and that's exactly what he did."

"Rider!" Arnie bellowed in agony, tearing off after him with his sword.

This was it: Eugene's big finish. He held his sword high and ran toward the rope, preparing to catch it and swing down to the lower level. He could already imagine the boys' raucous applause. He leaped for the rope, catching it effortlessly as he held his sword high in the air.

What he didn't count on was the momentum at that speed as his legs swung out at full force.

Before Eugene could even utter the words "The end," his foot accidentally went right through the window, causing the rest of the boys to scream.

Seconds later, the dormitory door flew open. A woman stood in the shadows. "EUGENE!"

Eugene cringed.

Her face tightened as she spied the broken window. Then she sighed. "Not again!"

TWO ⊙

Miss Clare stood in the doorway, wearing her nightdress and robe, her short white hair in curlers, looking like she had been woken from a deep sleep. She was a short, stocky woman, and Eugene and Arnwaldo already towered over her. She looked from the shattered glass to Eugene to the boys out of bed, and her mouth curved into a deep frown.

"Eugene," she moaned. "This is the third window you've broken this month."

"To be fair, the second window was not my fault." Eugene grabbed a broom and started sweeping up the mess. "Who knew teaching the boys how to juggle potatoes could be so dangerous?"

She sighed deeply. "How are we going to pay for this, boys?"

Arnie and Eugene looked at each other. *We.* Even if it was Eugene's fault, she'd never leave him hanging like that. Miss Clare treated all the boys in the orphanage like family.

"Maybe Lance Archer will give us money for a new window," Leif piped up.

"Yeah! Lance has come through for us before!" Rolf agreed.

"No one knows for sure the money on our doorstep was from him," argued Hugo, a boy who liked to argue over *everything*. "Lance Archer is a myth! No one has even seen him."

"I have," Arnie whispered loud enough for Eugene to hear.

At least Arnie *thought* he had. The way Eugene remembered the story, it was last summer and Arnie was outside on window-washing duty when an arrow narrowly whizzed past his head. When he looked up, the arrow was pinned to the orphanage door and a bag of much-needed coins was attached to it. Arnie had said that when he turned around he saw a large man wearing a bandana disappearing into the shadows. Arnie had been a Lance Archer fan ever since.

"Whether Lance Archer is real or not doesn't matter," Miss Clare said, sounding frustrated. "He doesn't know about our financial predicament or our broken window, and we can't wait around hoping this mythical man will find out. We need to fix this window now." She looked at the broken glass forlornly.

Eugene spoke up. "I'll offer to do some chores for Mr. Nilsen in exchange for a new window." The craftsman was always looking for extra apprentices in his shoppe, so it wouldn't be too hard to get work.

"So will I," Arnie chimed in. "Between the two of us working, we'll have a new window installed by end of day tomorrow."

Eugene fist-bumped his friend. Arnie always had his back.

"Thank you. Replacing the window is a good start, but you still need to be punished for your behavior," Miss Clare said sternly. "You two are the oldest. I count on you both to be an example to the others." They hung their heads. "First thing tomorrow, you'll both clean my office before breakfast."

Arnie groaned. "That early?"

Neither boy enjoyed rising with the sun. "I'll do it, Miss Clare,"

Eugene said. "Arnie doesn't have to. It wasn't his foot that hit the window."

"That's very thoughtful, Eugene, but since I caught both of you holding swords, and neither of you ever does anything without the other, I'll assume you were both involved here." Her eyes glinted mischievously. "Tomorrow morning, first thing, my office."

"Yes, ma'am," Arnie and Eugene said in unison.

"Now get to bed," Miss Clare said, turning around. "All of you. It's getting late."

There were more groans from the others, but they quickly fell in line, overturning chairs, closing hatches, and wrapping up ropes. Miss Clare, Eugene, and Arnie helped the younger boys climb into beds and hammocks hanging from the walls.

"You can have my quilt tonight, Marius," Eugene said, still feeling guilty about the window. The kid was always freezing, even in the summer. "You were sniffling all day."

"Thanks, Eugene," Marius said as he was being tucked in.

Arnie tossed his extra pillow to Rolf, whose arm was in a sling from a fall a week back. "And you can take my extra pillow to prop up your arm. It will heal faster."

"You're the best, Arnie," said Rolf with a yawn.

Miss Clare looked pleased as she watched the two of them. "I want you both to promise me — no more roughhousing," she whispered as the first of the boys in the room started to snore. "It's not behavior we want to teach here."

"Yes, ma'am," they said in unison.

Miss Clare put a hand on each of their cheeks. "But . . . since you do seem sorry . . ."

Eugene's face lit up. "We are!"

"And you helped get the others to bed . . ." Miss Clare added.

"We did. I gave away my pillow," Arnie reminded her.

Miss Clare smirked. She had a soft spot for both boys. When Eugene appeared on her orphanage doorstep with no name, she'd even named him after her father. "It's so hard to stay mad at you two! All right, you can both still sleep on the roof tonight as promised."

Eugene and Arnie silently cheered.

"As long as you're quiet," Miss Clare warned, and they nodded. "Just make sure you bring a blanket. It's chilly."

"Thanks, Miss Clare," Eugene said, and both boys hugged her before gathering their things.

They slipped through a hidden panel behind the painting of the kingdom's king and queen on the wall. Inside was a ladder that would take them straight up to the roof. The boys had discovered the passageway ages ago, but neither knew what the compartment was first used for. Some said the orphanage was originally a grain mill and that's why it still sometimes smelled like wheat. Whatever it was, all the ropes, hiding spots, and nooks were great for hideouts.

Arnie inhaled deeply as he popped through the hatch onto the roof. "This is what I'm talking about. Look at those stars."

Eugene pulled himself up. The sky was brilliant. A smattering of stars dotted the royal-blue sky as the moon bathed their small village in light. If Eugene looked to his right, he could just make out the soft glow coming from the castle in the distance. He imagined the king and queen were fast asleep, dreaming of the day they'd find their lost princess, who had been missing for almost five years. Eugene's heart gave a lurch whenever he thought about the girl.

Arnie had already laid his blanket down and spread out on top of it. "I bet if I started counting stars, I'd fall asleep before I finished."

Eugene put his blanket down next to him. "Don't count, then. I'm not ready to sleep yet. Are you?"

"No!" Arnie said. "It's way too early for that."

They were always getting in trouble for being up after curfew, talking about everything and anything — from the boat they were trying to build, to the complex recipes Arnie wanted Miss Clare to let him try in the kitchen (he loved to cook, and Eugene loved to eat, so it was a good combination).

"What'd you think of acting out the book tonight? Fun, right? I think the boys liked your Deserio bit," Eugene said as he focused on a particularly bright star. "I wasn't half bad either."

Arnie put his hands behind his head. "Remind me to never get between you and a spotlight."

Eugene pretended to be offended. "Can I help it if our audience loved me?" He attempted a sly grin. "With a face like this, how could they not." Arnie made an indistinguishable noise. "Hey! I heard that. What? Is it my nose? It's fine now, isn't it?"

Eugene couldn't help but think of that unfortunate incident last year. He'd been trying to show off for a few of the boys by proving he could walk across one of the loft beams — *blindfolded* (his idea). He was three-quarters of the way across (according to Arnie) before the fall. Miss Clare nearly passed out at the sight of his nose. He was never exactly sure if it set right afterward.

"Stop worrying," Arnie said. "You're a beaut! Someday everyone in this kingdom is going to know your name."

"Yes they will!" Eugene leaned back, satisfied.

"You'll be the next Flynn Rider, and I'll be . . ." He frowned. "I'm not sure. Arnwaldo Schnitz doesn't exactly roll off the tongue."

Eugene made a face. "No. Not that Eugene Fitzherbert is much better, but don't tell Miss Clare I said that," he added hastily.

"Never." Arnie looked at his friend. "Look, I don't care what people call us. I'm just glad we're in this together."

"Me too," Eugene said softly. He couldn't imagine his life without his best friend. "You're the closest thing I have to a family."

"The whole orphanage is our family," Arnie corrected him. "And it's a great family to have, so don't get all sad on me again and start talking about finding your parents."

"You're right," Eugene agreed, even though he could talk about wanting to find his parents every day of the week, twenty-four hours a day. But maybe that was because he knew they were out there somewhere. He'd arrived at Miss Clare's Home for Boys with a note, which he snuck down to read in Miss Clare's office whenever he could. Arnie, however, had been brought to the orphanage after his parents fell ill and died soon after he was born. He'd arrived just a few months before Eugene. Miss Clare said they'd been inseparable ever since. "I know we've got a great family right here . . . but don't you ever worry about us getting too old to stay? I don't know any orphans who lived here past twelve."

When Eugene thought back to older boys who'd left at his age, he remembered Hammond becoming an apprentice for the blacksmith and Peter going to work on a farm. Miss Clare never pressed him or Arnie about their future plans, but she probably expected them to at least be thinking about them. If they hadn't been adopted by this point, chances were it wasn't happening. Besides, Eugene didn't want to be adopted. His parents were still out there. He had proof of that. He just had to find them.

"Miss Clare loves us," Arnie argued. "We're a huge help to her."

"When we aren't breaking windows."

"When *you* aren't breaking windows," Arnie teased, and Eugene punched his arm. "She'd never ask us to leave, but when *we* want to go, we'll have the boat ready to sail off to destinations unknown."

"Too bad the boat is still only a rowboat with a pile of scrap wood sitting in it."

"There's no rush to finish it," Arnie said. "We have plenty of time."

Did they? Eugene didn't want to say anything, but Arnie turned thirteen in four months. What happened then? What if Miss Clare couldn't keep them around anymore? If Arnie had to go, Eugene would, too. But where? Without the boat, they had no future and no way of getting around the world (and finding his family). They had to get that boat done.

"Maybe when we work for Mr. Nilsen to get the window fixed, we can see if he has some scrap we can use to finish the bow of the ship," Eugene said, getting excited. "Then we can figure out how to get a sail and we're golden! We'll be sailing in no time." Arnie was quiet as he looked at the night sky. "Think about it! We'll sail to someplace with good work, make a ton of money, and never have to worry about needing anything ever again. Just imagine the adventures we'll have. They'll be better than any of Rider's!"

"Definitely," said Arnie, but he didn't sound convinced.

That was okay. This is what best friends were for — building each other up and helping each other see the silver linings.

"I'm thinking once we have enough money saved up, we can buy a bigger boat that we can live on full-time," Eugene added. "Then we'll just sail all around the world, selling the treasures we find, and then . . ."

Once Eugene got started about the future, there was no stopping him. Arnie nodded along until he finally dozed off. That's when Eugene started to write his life story.

"Eugene Fitzherbert couldn't believe his eyes," he whispered as Arnie snored beside him. "He'd sailed thousands of miles and visited dozens of shores, and finally he'd found them. 'Mother? Father?' he said as his parents opened their arms wide and embraced him. 'We've been looking for you for years!' his father said. 'We'd almost given up hope till we saw your ship come into port, and then we just knew it was you.' Eugene clung to them, happy to finally be reunited with the family he'd searched everywhere to find. The end."

Eugene smiled to himself. It was a good story. Some dreams were worth waiting for.

The next morning, the two boys woke with the sun just as the village was beginning to stir. Eugene could see Mr. Kaas opening the doors to his bakery, while down the road Miss Hacke was sweeping in front of the market. The Boyle brothers were walking several horses from a nearby stable to the farm.

"Wow, you smell that bread?" Arnie inhaled deeply. "Mr. Kaas must be making cinnamon loaves. I really hope he burns the bottoms again."

All half-burnt baked goods went straight to the orphanage. Once they cut away the charred pieces, the bread tasted good enough. "Me too. Filip is on cooking duty again, and you know what that means."

"Sludge," the boys said at the same time.

Filip never added enough milk to the bowl, which meant the porridge was as thick as mud and stuck to the roof of your mouth.

"Guess we should get downstairs to Miss Clare's office and get started." Eugene stretched his arms. "If we're lucky, the sludge will be gone by lunch."

"Good plan," Arnie agreed, rolling up his blanket. He stood on the roof and looked out. "Hey. What's that long line of carriages coming this way? Are the king and queen visiting?"

Eugene stood up and squinted in the sunlight. "We would have heard about that. Besides, I don't think the king and queen travel with elephants."

A line of at least eight wagons with burlap covers were headed down the winding road that led into the village, trailed by a line of animals traveling on foot. The boys watched as the caravan stopped near the outskirts of town. Several men jumped off the wagons and started unloading supplies.

"What are they up to?" Arnie said. "That's what I want to know."

"Guess we'll find out soon enough," Eugene said. "Nothing stays quiet in the kingdom for long. Let's get to work."

And by work, Eugene meant snooping. How could he pass up the chance to read Miss Clare's papers when she left them right out in the open? Miss Clare's office was small but mostly tidy, with a small table and chairs used for talks with prospective parents. Artwork by the boys hung on two walls, along with a painting of Miss Clare's beloved niece, Kathryn, who lived on the other side of the kingdom.

"Can you stop reading Miss Clare's stuff and help me sweep already? We're never going to get out of here at this rate," Arnie grumbled. "Eugene? What's that paper say, anyway?"

Eugene wasn't sure he had the heart to say the words aloud. "Someone wants to adopt Marius."

Arnie's arm waffled slightly, but he caught the broom before it fell. "Are you sure?"

Eugene placed the papers back down exactly as they'd been so she wouldn't suspect he'd read them. "It says 'Petition to Adopt' right on top. It's a young couple that lives right outside the village; they're looking for a boy under the age of ten to join two other brothers."

"Good for Marius," Arnie said softly. "He'll make a good big brother."

"Yeah." He was happy for Marius, but his heart still ached. "Remember how he taught himself to tie his boots by making up a song about it?"

"You pull the left string tight and loop over the right, then you give them both a tug till the loop becomes snug . . ." Arnie sang. "All the boys were singing it. Drove me nuts." He started to chuckle. Eugene joined in. Then their laughter faded. "I'm going to miss that kid."

"Me too." Eugene stared at the tiny specks of dust visible in the sunlight streaming through the window. Familiar, unpleasant thoughts started to creep in. Another kid was getting adopted and he was still here, no closer to finding his parents. He tried to think of something to say to lighten the mood. "Hey. With Marius leaving, it might be nice if we did another live reading. We could do his favorite Rider book. What do you say to performing *Calypso Cove* tonight?"

Arnie groaned. "We haven't even paid off the window you broke last night and you want to try this again?"

"We'll be more careful," Eugene promised. "Look how well we treated Miss Clare's office. This place is spotless!" He saw a piece of red string peeking out from the closet door. "Except for that." He gave the string a yank, but it wouldn't budge. Eugene opened the door to see what it was caught on and found a whole ball of yarn, which he picked up. His eyes instinctively wandered over to the shelves.

Arnie dropped the broom and came running. "Oh no. You get out of there right now."

This was Miss Clare's keepsake closet for the boys. Whether it was a letter from the parents who gave one of the boys up, the blanket they came wrapped in, or a shirt they arrived wearing, Miss Clare held on to their items till the day they left her care. Eugene's eyes traveled up to a basket on the second shelf.

Arnie groaned. "I mean it, Eugene. No good ever comes of this. Eugene?"

Eugene's hand instinctively went to the basket second to the right with a blue label marked E.F. He reached past the small faded blue blanket and went for the yellowed envelope with the faded handwriting. *Dear Sir or Madam* he read inside his head. He knew the letter by heart.

Dear Sir or Madam,

This child is special! More special than I can put into words. He's been through a lot already, so take good care of him. His family asked that I look after him for the time being, but unfortunately my new employment leaves me with little time to care for a small child. Till they can return for him, please give him the best home possible. And tell him that he is fiercely loved. Wherever he journeys, these books should travel with him. They were passed down from his parents. May they make him smile, even on the darkest of days like this one.

—M

No matter how many times Eugene read the note, he still had the same questions: Who was M? His mother? If his parents left him the Flynn Rider books, then they must have meant something to them. And the note said he was fiercely loved. So what happened to his parents to make them ask M to look after him? And why was this M writing about dark days? What had he been through that led to him winding up in Miss Clare's Home for Boys?

Miss Clare didn't have the answers. She didn't even see who placed Eugene on her doorstep. All she had of his former life were his books, a blanket, and this note written on a piece of parchment with no letterhead or signature. There was, however, a strange symbol etched at the bottom. It was a circular shape with three dashes that looked like whiskers. Try as Eugene might, he didn't know what the symbol was or what it stood for. Often, when the boys were doing schoolwork, Eugene would search books for the symbol, but he always turned up empty-handed. The mark was a complete mystery, as was his past.

Arnie's voice pierced Eugene's thoughts. "Miss Clare is going to be checking on us soon. She's going to be upset if she catches you in here again."

Upset? Yes. Mad? No. Miss Clare knew he longed to know where he was from. They had spent many hours in front of the fire, talking about family and what that word meant. "The saying 'blood is thicker than water,' is hogwash," Miss Clare liked to tell him. "Family is the one you make for yourself along the way. It's the people who know and love you for who you really are. That's your real family. You don't need adoption papers to prove that."

"A family is the one you make for yourself," Arnie said now, as if hearing his thoughts.

Eugene looked over at his best friend. Arnie knew Eugene spent too much time in front of the mirror trying to tame his cowlick, that he loved apples and hated oranges, and that his favorite time of day was sunrise. And Eugene knew Arnie loved to cook, hated spiders, and longed for the day he could pierce his ear like Lance Archer supposedly had (Archer had an earring in all his WANTED poster sketches). Too bad Miss Clare would never allow it. Arnie may have been content at the orphanage, but Eugene couldn't get his parents out of his head. He would find them, and when he did, Arnie would come live with them, too. Arnie was also his family in every sense of the word.

"I know, but this symbol . . . whenever I see it on this letter, it makes me think it's there for a reason. Like it's a clue to finding my parents." Eugene looked at Arnie hopefully. "Why else put it on the paper?"

Arnie peered over his shoulder again. "Maybe M was just trying to draw a cat and forgot the eyes. And the nose. And the mouth."

There was a jingling sound, and suddenly they heard voices.

"If you would just come this way, you'll find my quarters much more comfortable," Miss Clare could be heard saying.

"Time to move!" Eugene hissed, putting the letter back in the envelope, the envelope back behind the blanket, and the basket back on the shelf.

Arnie ran to the door, saw the doorknob turning, and looked back at Eugene. "We're trapped! Only way out now is the window."

But there was no time to get to the window, so Eugene did the only thing he could think of. He grabbed Arnie's arm and yanked him back into the closet, closing the door quietly behind them.

"Now, Mr. Frost, before we get down to business, you must sit for a spell and have a proper cup of tea," Miss Clare told the man, who towered over her by at least two feet. "I made the peppermint especially for you."

"For me?" Kurtis asked. "Why? Have I said I liked peppermint before?"

Miss Clare looked flustered. "Why, yes, I believe you mentioned it last time you were here when I had no peppermint to serve you. That's why you declined to stay."

"Ah." Kurtis's coal-like eyes lit up. "Well, I no longer like peppermint, so I fear I won't be able to join you this time either."

Don't let him get to you, Miss Clare, Eugene thought. *Who would want to have tea with this guy anyway?*

"Oh, well." Miss Clare sighed. "How about a cookie? Do you like chocolate chip? The children made these yesterday."

Kurtis trailed his finger along the table, looking for dust, of which there was none on account of Eugene's expert dusting, so *ha!* "As I've told you before, Miss Clare, you are one of many stops during my day. I don't have time to sit and pass pleasantries. I am here to collect your taxes."

Eugene clenched his fists. No one treated the nicest little old lady in the kingdom like this.

Miss Clare pursed her lips. "Yes. About that. It seems the money sent to me by the royal family hasn't yet arrived this month."

Kurtis picked up a cookie and took a bite. "And . . . ?"

"Well, as you know, Mr. Frost, the money Miss Clare's Home for Boys receives from the kingdom keeps us afloat. The money I make from sewing barely covers the groceries for all these growing boys." She chuckled to herself. "Especially when one of them accidentally breaks a window during an impromptu performance."

THREE

**"PLAYING BY THE RULES ALL THE TIME
CAN GET KIND OF BORING."**

—Flynnigan Rider in *Flynnigan Rider and the Buried Treasure*

"Here we are!" they heard Miss Clare say even though couldn't see her. Her body was being blocked by a figure. "Please have a seat."

Eugene and Arnie jockeyed for position in front of the dark closet keyhole. Eugene couldn't figure out who Miss Clare talking to.

"I don't think that will be necessary," said a deep voice.

The figure slowly turned to face the closet, and Eugene recogniz the man with the mustache immediately. It was Kurtis Frost, the sc of the kingdom: their tax collector. When it came to payment, y either had the money owed or you felt his wrath.

Kurtis drifted around the room, picking up papers that didn belong to him, which Eugene considered *his* job. Kurtis didn't get t do that! Or stare at the kids' artwork. Eugene wanted the guy gone His whole demeanor and look — tall, dark hair and eyes, a perennially stormy expression, and strange attire (he always wore a snug sweater regardless of the season) — just felt wrong.

Eugene felt his face burn.

"Broken window?" Kurtis looked at her. "I'm afraid I don't understand what this has to do with me."

"Well, last night — "

Kurtis cut her off. "I don't need an explanation. What I need is the money you owe the kingdom."

"I know, and I promise I'll pay it as soon as the check arrives." Miss Clare smiled brightly. "I'm terribly sorry it is late, but you know I always pay, and to be fair, you *are* here two days early. Perhaps you could swing by us later on your journey? I'm sure the gold coins we owe will be here before you return."

"I don't have time to make a return trip, Miss Clare," he said curtly. "I am trying to throw that Lance Archer off my scent and do my collections early. He's hit me twice the past few months."

At the mention of Lance, Arnie pushed Eugene aside to listen better.

"Taking tax money from our king to give to the poor," Kurtis fumed. "It's just outrageous! I can't let it continue, hence the early arrival for taxes. Surely you have money tucked away."

Miss Clare's brow crinkled with worry. "No. I'm sorry. I barely have enough to cover the food for the week, let alone the taxes. If I give you all I have before the stipend arrives, the children will starve."

"Miss Clare." Kurtis tsked. "This sounds like poor finances to me."

Eugene gripped the doorknob tight to keep from screaming. Sometimes he wondered if Mr. Frost got a kick out of making Miss Clare squirm.

"A person should always have money for a rainy day, especially when they are responsible for a group of children!" Kurtis continued. Eugene watched a calm come over the man. "Unless . . . Is it possible you misplaced it?"

"No!" Miss Clare sounded outraged. "I would never misplace money from our king."

"Everyone in the village who gets funding from the king had their tax money this morning. Are you certain you haven't forgotten that it arrived?" He picked up a cookie and took a bite, made a face, then put the rest on a napkin. "At your age, it wouldn't be unheard of."

Eugene inhaled sharply. Miss Clare was not too old! Sure, she forgot where her knitting needles were sometimes, but that was because the boys were always stealing them to use as swords.

"I am not too old to run this place, if that's what you're insinuating, Mr. Frost."

He ignored her and placed a hand on one of the wood beams that ran along parts of the walls and ceiling. "Perhaps it's this demanding job and the upkeep of this big, old building . . ." He gave her a pitiful look. "You deserve to retire at your advanced age. This home doesn't service that many boys anymore. Surely they can be reassigned elsewhere, and this place could be put to better use."

Miss Clare put down her teacup. "Reassigned? My boys are not going anywhere!" Her voice grew shrill. "What are you saying?"

"Clearly the stress of managing money is getting to be too much for you." Kurtis smiled thinly and took out his quill to write something down on his papers. "Yes, I think that will be my recommendation when I next see the king. He should close Miss Clare's Home for Boys and send each child elsewhere."

Eugene burst out of the closet before Miss Clare could even react. "Hang on right there, Mr. Frosty!" Arnie fell out of the closet behind him, and Miss Clare looked at them both in surprise. "You know, because of your last name and everything and, uh . . . nice sweater."

Kurtis's face flushed with anger, and Eugene started to second-guess himself.

"Were you two spying on me?" Kurtis hissed. "Who are you?"

He was already in trouble. Why not cement his fate and tell the guy what he really thought of him? "I am Eugene Fitzherbert, but that doesn't matter. What matters is who you are!" He pointed his finger at Kurtis's chest. "You're a crook and a liar and . . . and . . ." Eugene tried to think of something harsher to say. "Actually your sweater is way too small for a man of your size. Did you knit it yourself?" Eugene touched a loose thread and pulled. The sweater began to unravel. "Oops! This is why you should have Miss Clare knit for you." Arnie snorted.

"Eugene!" Miss Clare inhaled sharply.

"Why, I've never been treated so poorly in my life!" Kurtis's face turned even redder. "If this is how you're raising these urchins, then I'm even further convinced it's time for you to retire, Miss Clare!"

Eugene paled. He'd made the situation worse.

Kurtis turned to Miss Clare. "I'll be reporting this to the king. And I expect that money — *with interest* — in one week, or there will be a price to pay, Miss Clare. Good day!"

"Wait! Mr. Frost . . . I — " But Kurtis stormed out of the apartment before Miss Clare could even shuffle to the door.

Miss Clare spun around, her hands on her face. "Oh, boys, what have you done?"

"That didn't go exactly as I planned," Eugene said meekly. "You see . . ."

"I don't want to hear it!" Miss Clare raised her voice, which she never, ever did. "Mr. Frost is going to report us to the *king*! Oh my." She covered her face with her hands again. "What are we going to do?"

Now Eugene felt awful. He and Arnie walked over to Miss Clare and put their arms around her.

"Miss Clare, it's going to be okay," Arnie said soothingly. "You said the coins will be here any day, right?"

She lowered her hands. Her eyes were red. "They should have been here by now. It always arrives by the twentieth of the month, but this time it didn't come. I don't know . . . Do you think Lance Archer somehow got ahold of it?"

"He'd never take from an orphanage," Arnie said firmly.

"Maybe you should send word to the king, just to make sure they sent the money out already," Eugene suggested.

"I thought of that, but then I heard from someone in the village that the king has been cutting back aid to some folk." She frowned. "What if our home is no longer a priority and I have to send you all away?"

Eugene watched Arnie scratch his left eyebrow. He only did that when he was nervous. And talk of the orphanage possibly shutting down was enough to make both of them nervous. "Don't you worry about that mean old crook," he told Miss Clare. "The coins are coming. I can feel it!" He looked at Arnie for backup. "I promise, someday you won't even have to worry about money. Arnie and I are going to finish our boat and sail out of here, and when we do, we'll earn so much we'll make sure this place grows to twice the size with twice as many kids."

Arnie grinned, his worries forgotten. "Yes! Miss Clare, you are never going to have to worry about money ever again!"

Eugene could almost see it. With the money they got her, Miss Clare could build an even bigger orphanage for all the kids who needed a place to stay. They'd each have thick mattresses, heavy quilts on the beds, shelves of books, and actual porridge instead of sludge. It would be incredible.

Miss Clare started to laugh. "I like the sound of that, boys." She patted their arms. "And I don't want you to worry about the money. We will figure it out. You two go see Mr. Nilsen about that window and let me worry about the rest."

"Yes, ma'am," they said in unison.

"Calling my boys urchins . . ." Miss Clare shuffled over to her desk, shaking her head. "I should really report *him* to the king. In fact, I'm going to write him right now. I'll take care of this matter so we can focus on happy things like the circus coming to town."

"Circus? What's a circus?" Eugene asked.

Miss Clare's face lit up. "Oh, it's wonderful! I went to one years ago. The performers do all sorts of acts. This one is called *The Great Baron and His Unusual Oddities*! They've been setting up outside town all morning."

"That's what that caravan was!" Arnie said.

"So it's a show," Eugene said, understanding. "And they perform for us?" This was an idea he could get behind.

"Yes." Miss Clare smiled and ushered them both to the door. "And it's going to change your life. I promise you!"

FOUR

"I KNOW NOT WHO YOU ARE, NOR HOW I CAME TO FIND YOU,
BUT MAY I JUST SAY . . . HI. HOW YA DOIN'?
THE NAME'S FLYNN. FLYNN RIDER."

—FLYNNIGAN RIDER IN *THE TALES OF FLYNNIGAN RIDER*

As Eugene and the other orphans headed out to the parade route the next morning, everyone was buzzing about the circus. It was the biggest thing to come through the village since the royal processional after the princess's birth, which Eugene was far too young to remember himself.

"I heard they have a dragon," Eugene overheard the blacksmith's apprentice say as he walked alongside the village baker.

"I heard they have magic tricks!" the baker exclaimed. "And we get to see it all for free!"

Eugene turned to Arnie as some kids ran by chattering about seeing an elephant outside town. "I have a question: When is anything in the village ever free?"

"Never. This circus thing must have some sort of catch." Arnie played with the tight collar on his dress shirt. Miss Clare had made the boys dress in their finest clothes for the occasion, and no one was loving the constricting attire.

Eugene turned to the shoppe window behind him and checked

out his reflection in the glass for the umpteenth time. Should his hair be more poufy? Which way did his part look best? Was his shirt supposed to be buttoned up tight or half-open? And how was he actually supposed to smile? He attempted different grins in the glass, unsure of the right one. Was his smile too wide? Not wide enough? Maybe it worked better if he smoothed his hair down, kept his mouth closed, and attempted Flynn Rider's famous smolder. He bit his lower lip, lowered his chin, and raised his eyes to the glass.

Arnie burst out laughing. "What are you doing?"

"Trying to figure out my look." Eugene tried to act confident, but inside he felt ridiculous. "Which one do you like?" He messed up his hair again and tried the smolder, then smoothed his hair down and gave Arnie a wide grin.

"Geez, Eugene, I don't know. Just be you."

That was the problem. Eugene wasn't sure who he was yet.

"Please clear the way!" called out the captain of the royal guard. He was riding down the street on horseback as other guards followed close behind. "The circus will be coming through shortly!"

Eugene turned and stood next to Arnie. The village was more crowded than Eugene had ever seen it. Festive spruce garlands and purple flags adorned with the official emblem of the kingdom—a gold sunburst—hung across the dirt road connected by thatched cottages. Someone nearby was playing a lute while shopkeepers with market carts sold various foods like roasted chestnuts. His eyes stayed on the edge of town for any sign of the circus. So far he saw none. Just a lot of people two or three deep lined up in front of the shoppes, watching nothing happen.

"Where are they already?" whined a small child from atop his father's shoulder.

"They'll be here any minute," promised his mother.

Marius tugged on Eugene's pant leg. "Can you see it? Can you?"

"Not you, too!" He ruffled the hair on Marius's head. "Believe me, little man, when something is happening, you will be the first to know. Right now all I can see is Arnie's big head blocking my view of the bakery cart."

"As if you had money for a muffin anyway," Arnie grumbled.

"True, but it would still be nice to *see*." He loved his boots, but they were two sizes too big, and flat, which meant they gave him no height.

Suddenly, a trumpet sounded and the crowd began to cheer.

Three trumpeters in red velvet suits appeared, with acrobats doing somersaults trailing closely behind. They were closely followed by two jesters carrying a gold post with a sign that read THE GREAT BARON AND HIS UNUSUAL ODDITIES! Six horses with riders sitting in various poses came next. One was even doing a handstand! Then the caravan appeared.

Eugene counted seven wagons rumbling over the cobblestones. The crowd went wild when they saw them. Every single driver was tossing out candy and trinkets! Eugene hoisted Marius up onto his shoulders, and the kid caught a small wooden kazoo. He quickly put it in his mouth and began blowing as loudly as he could.

"Look! More animals!" Filip shouted as wheeled cages filled with lizards, poodles, and other small creatures he didn't even recognize rolled by. They were followed by a group of ponies that walked with geese perched atop their backs. Eugene had never seen such a spectacle.

"Wow" said Marius. "The circus is amazing!"

Wow was right. Eugene snuck a glance at Arnie, who looked as starstruck as he felt.

A drum started to beat in the distance, and people timed their claps with the sound. Two drummers appeared, kicking up dirt as they followed in the path of the others. "Make way for the Great Baron!" one shouted.

That's when the biggest, nicest-looking wagon of all appeared. A young man in a blue velvet suit, looking as regal as a king, sat atop it. *That must be the Baron*, Eugene presumed. The guy was all muscle, which was evident through the fitted jacket he was wearing. He smiled dazzlingly as he played with a long, blond mustache that had been waxed and curled at the ends. But it was the flowing blond hair that grazed his shoulders that was the real showstopper. How did he get it to look so tousled and shiny?

A girl around Eugene's age poked her head out of the wagon and whispered something in the Baron's ear. She noticed Eugene staring and gave him a shy smile, which made Eugene stand up straighter and puff out his chest. The Baron pulled his wagon to a stop and stood up. "For your own safety, we need your silence as we bring in this next wagon!" he said in a deep, commanding voice.

Safety? People around Eugene shuffled uncomfortably and whispered as a wagon wrapped in chains rolled up alongside the Baron. On the carriage was a sign that read: *BEWARE! DRAGON! DON'T PROVOKE!*

"Dragon? How did they capture a real dragon?" Marius asked nervously.

"And what's 'provoke' mean?" Filip asked, looking equally uneasy.

"It means don't try to make it angry," said Eugene. "But I wouldn't worry. There is no way they're keeping a fire-breathing dragon in a wooden box. Unless they want to turn this parade into a bonfire!" He made eye contact with Arnie, and they both laughed uneasily.

And that was before they heard a low menacing moan coming from inside the wagon.

Shrieks arose from the crowd as the wagon began to buck and shake. The rest of the caravan stopped short, and two boys not much older than Eugene jumped off the carriage, brandishing mace weapons.

"Maybe we should go," Eugene heard a mother say. People next to him began pushing their way out of the crowd.

"Do not fear!" said the Baron, climbing down from his wagon. "I can tame the creature." He pulled a whip out of the holster at his waist and flicked it at the wagon. "Silence, beast!" The bucking wagon immediately went still.

The crowd cheered. The Baron and the two boys bowed, then resumed their positions atop the carriages. Eugene noticed that the two boys, however, kept their maces at the ready as they rode past.

Man, do they look cool. I wonder if that's heavy, Eugene thought, suddenly picturing himself in a fighting stance, holding a more elegant weapon such as a sword.

"Eugene!" Arnie poked him in the ribs. "Did you see those guys? They look like they're our age, and they're taming dragons!"

"I wonder how they got that gig." Eugene scratched his chin and thought about how he'd look if he grew a mustache and had a mace.

"Experience a small taste of the Great Baron and His Unusual Oddities!" cried a jester as the last of the ponies and the acrobats came down the street. "For a nominal fee, you can also experience other thrills of a lifetime! Ticket sales straight ahead."

As if under a spell, the crowd moved like a herd toward the wagons, which had formed a semicircle in the town square.

"Can we go?" asked Leif. "Miss Clare said we don't have to be home till supper."

"But we don't have money for tickets," Filip pointed out.

Eugene looked at Arnie. "I'm sure there will still be stuff to look at. Let's check it out." He put Marius down and took the small boy's hand, the smell of something sweet, as well as curiosity, pulling him forward.

By the time they reached the square, the circus had already set up. They had everything from a petting zoo to a magician performing tricks. In another area, a blindfolded, beefy man with a hook for a hand was throwing axes at a bull's-eye!

"There's the dragon," Marius whispered, pointing at the chained wagon. A huge crowd was already forming around it. The Great Baron stood alongside it, snapping his whip. Eugene watched as person after person in line handed over a silver coin, then stepped up to take a peek at the dragon through a hole in the fabric. The next woman in line peered inside and shrieked.

"It was huge!" she exclaimed, rushing past Eugene. "And all that smoke!"

"I want to see, too," Filip moaned.

"So do I," Marius said sadly. "I wish we had coins."

Eugene hated seeing the kids upset. Soon, Marius would be adopted and with a new family. They only had a few days left together, and he wanted to make sure Marius didn't forget him. Spying the ticket wagon, he noticed the girl who had been sitting with the Baron. "I have an idea. Come on, Marius. Everybody follow me."

Arnie gave him a look. "What are you up to? Eugene?"

But Eugene didn't answer. He had to concentrate. He jumped into line and breathed in and out slowly, practicing in his head. *Be like Rider. Be like Rider.* How hard could it be? He knew the lines by heart. He'd said them a thousand times! When it was finally his turn, he approached the pretty girl with a smile. "I know not who you are, nor how I came to find you, but may I just say . . . hi." He leaned one arm on the wagon and smiled brighter. This move always worked for Rider.

The girl looked at him curiously. "Um . . . hi? How many tickets do you want?"

Shouldn't she be swooning by now? He was a good-looking guy, wasn't he? Sure, Rider had, like, thirty pounds of muscle and four inches of height on him, but Eugene bathed. He didn't smell. He attempted to keep well groomed, which the other boys were always making fun of him for, and his too-tight dress shirt was clean. He could dazzle this girl if given the chance! He just had to keep going. He cleared his throat hoping his squeaky voice sounded deeper. "How ya doin'? The name's Flynn. Flynn Rider."

She smiled thinly. She had very nice cheekbones and the longest lashes he'd ever seen. "Welcome, Flynn Rider," she said. "My name is Staylan." Her smile disappeared. "And if you can't buy a ticket, then we have nothing left to talk about. NEXT!"

"But . . ." Why hadn't the move worked? Maybe he needed to attempt the smolder again. He scrunched up his face real tight, bit his lower lip, and tried to bat his eyes at her.

She glanced worriedly at him. "You sick or something? Move on or I'll have the guys chase you out of here. We don't do handouts."

Desperate times called for desperate measures. "We're orphans," Eugene blurted out, pulling Marius and Filip in close. "Not a nickel to our names, and these two tykes right here would give anything to see that dragon you've got locked up." He tried batting his eyes at her again. "Is there any way you could find room in your heart to give us tickets?"

Staylan looked at them for a moment. "No." She turned to the crowd. "Who has money to buy a ticket? Step right up!"

Eugene moved aside, and Arnie started to laugh.

"Flynn Rider? Seriously? You thought she'd buy that?" Arnie held his stomach he was laughing so hard.

"I thought she'd let us in." Eugene's cheeks burned. "I think I even had her convinced for a moment." He pretended to stare at a WANTED poster on a nearby pole. It was for Lance Archer. This sketch made his gold earring look as big as his head. Who drew these things?

"Oooh! Look at the mime!" Marius said, all but forgetting about the dragon. He, Leif, and Rolf took off running.

"Hey, did you say you guys are orphans?" A boy in a red velvet vest holding a cage with a chameleon approached them. "So am I. Herford Home for Boys. You?"

"Miss Clare's Home for Boys," Arnie said. "You work for the circus?"

The boy nodded. "Past two years. Best years of my life." He held out his hand. "I'm Andy."

"Uh, my friends call me Lance." Arnie side-eyed Eugene. "And this here is my friend Eu— *Flynn*," he corrected himself. "So you're an orphan, too?"

"Not anymore." Andy handed off the chameleon to the closest worker. "These guys are my family now. It's a good life. We spend our time on the road, moving from town to town, seeing new kingdoms and sunrises every other week. We're well-fed and make a living for ourselves."

Moving from kingdom to kingdom? Eugene's face lit up. "That sounds pretty perfect." He glanced at Arnie, who also looked mildly intrigued. Maybe they wouldn't need to finish the boat to travel the world! If they could do it with the circus, he'd find his parents in no time. But there was one other issue. "How much do you make?"

"Enough not to need handouts," Andy said with a lopsided grin. "I owe nobody and am owned by no one." He brushed a piece of lint off the shirt he was wearing, which looked brand-new. "There are some pretty good bonuses, too, if you catch my drift." He winked. "I can't talk about those here, but if you're interested, the Baron is always looking for loyal guys."

Bonuses? Eugene saw dollar signs. "We're definitely interested. Where can we find you after the show?"

"Flynn," Arnie said, looking uncomfortable.

"We set up camp out by the Selvag Mines," Andy told them. "Come by tonight. We always have a huge bonfire the night before the circus starts."

"What do you mean? Isn't *this* the circus?" Eugene asked.

Andy laughed. "Oh, this is just a teaser to get people excited and want to fork over money to see more. We're in this kingdom for the next two weeks, but the Baron usually only takes on new guys the first night so they have time for their initiation."

"Initiation?" Arnie sounded worried.

"It's nothing." Andy shrugged him off. "You guys look like you can handle it."

"Hey, Andy! Come on!" said a boy with a large nose and big teeth. "They need help with the tonic."

"Come by tonight!" Andy said as he ran off. "We'll show you around!"

"We will!" Eugene shouted as Andy disappeared into the crowd. He clapped Arnie on the back. "This is it! Our big break! Who knew I'd be discovered for my natural stage presence?"

"Eugene, what are you doing? We're not joining the circus . . . are we?" He scratched his left eyebrow, and Eugene knew he was definitely worked up.

He squeezed Arnie tight. "This might be the perfect gig for us, Arn! We can't stay with Miss Clare forever, and our boat is nowhere near done. What if this is our chance to get out there and see the world on our own terms and be a part of something amazing? I mean, how great is this circus thing?"

A mime with a white-painted face pretending to be trapped inside a box walked by them, and a man dropped a silver coin in his pocket. Just for pretending to be stuck!

"This morning you said the circus sounded like a sham," Arnie pointed out.

"That was before I saw how dazzling it is. Look how happy it's making everyone!"

"I know, but . . ." Arnie hesitated. "Are you really ready to leave the orphanage, Miss Clare, and all the boys? They're our family."

Eugene's smile faded. They'd always planned to go, but when Arnie put it that way, his heart was torn. This was beginning to feel very real. "I know," he said quietly. "But how long will our home even be here if Kurtis Frost gets his way?"

Arnie frowned. "Right . . . And if we get jobs, we could send money back to Miss Clare and help save our home."

"And there you have it — the perfect plan," Eugene agreed. They grinned at each other.

"Step right up!" shouted a redheaded boy with long sideburns. "Buy the tonic that's the buzz of every kingdom! Villagers everywhere want it, but you can only find it here at the Great Baron and His Unusual Oddities!"

Eugene turned to get a closer look. The boy was standing in front of a wagon stacked with crates full of tiny glass bottles. Each one contained a white liquid that sparkled in the sun. A wood cutout of a half-moon hung over the shelves.

"Drink from the fountain of youth and look decades younger!" Sideburns said. An identical boy with a patch on his left eye stood beside him, silent. "But be quick! This is our most popular item, and we only have this limited supply of tonic left. It's first come, first served."

Eugene and Arnie watched a crowd begin to gather.

"How do we know the tonic works?" asked a girl in the crowd. Eugene did a double take. It was Staylan.

"I'm glad you asked, young lady," said the boy. "We will show you. May we have a volunteer from the audience? They can test the tonic for free!"

"I'll do it!" An older man, with a long, white beard, shuffled forward, leaning on a cane. "Just give me a minute to get up there. This body doesn't work the way it used to." The crowd chuckled.

"That will change soon!" Sideburns handed over a glittering bottle. "Drink up!"

The man's hands were shaking as he popped the cork and took a big sip. He swallowed. Nothing happened for a moment. Suddenly the man started coughing wildly and doubled over, turning away from the crowd. Sideburns and his friend with the eye patch patted him on the back, and the man's coughing stopped.

When he turned to face the audience again, he flung his cane and tossed his cloak on the ground. The crowd gasped. Gone was the beard, the white hair, and the frail body. The man standing before them was fifty years younger!

"It's a miracle!" the man cried, and people applauded. "Look at me! What is this amazing elixir called?"

Sideburns grinned, revealing crooked teeth. "Moonstone drops."

"I'll take a bottle!" said someone in the crowd.

"Me too!" said another.

As people began pushing and shoving their way to the front, Eugene's oversized boots got the better of him. He fell hard, landing near a wagon wheel. Before he could be trampled, he put his hand on the wheel to pull himself up. That's when his eye caught sight of something. Underneath the carriage was a long white wig and a cape. Eugene quickly put two and two together. The man's transformation had been an act! The Great Baron was making a fortune from something that was probably nothing more than sugar water — and what a performance.

Clever.

He looked over at the redheaded boys again with renewed interest and watched as a few of the other circus men walked over to control the crowd. The largest man in the group pushed his way to the front and held up both hands. "Everyone step back!"

Eugene looked at the man's right bicep and inhaled sharply.

In the center of his bulging muscle was a tattoo: a circle with three whiskerlike slashes through it. Eugene knew exactly where he'd seen the symbol before: in his letter.

Could this man know his parents? His heart started drumming wildly.

He knew what he had to do: Tonight, he and Arnie would join the circus.

FĪVE

"YOU WANT TO SEE THE WORLD? TO DO THAT,
YOU'VE GOT TO GET OUT THERE AND LIVE IN IT."

—FLYNNIGAN RIDER IN *FLYNNIGAN RIDER AND THE LOST TREASURE OF SCOTIA*

Living in an orphanage, Eugene was used to saying good-bye. But tonight was the first time he'd be the one doing the leaving. He wasn't sure he had it in him to say the actual word, though. How did he say "good-bye" to boys who felt like brothers?

Even though the circus would be in the kingdom for the next few weeks and he might cross paths with the boys again, Eugene decided to do something they all would remember—a rousing final read-aloud of a Flynn tale. *Whoever picks up the bedtime ritual after we go will be nowhere as good,* he thought to himself.

"As Flynn mounted Oliver, his horse, he took one last lingering look back at the sleeping village," Eugene read aloud, the words sticking to him like a good goulash. "And he wondered again if he was making the right choice. His best mate, Nial, saddled up and rode alongside him. 'Having second thoughts?' Nial asked." Eugene looked for Arnie across the room, and he smiled encouragingly. "'No,' Flynn said. 'We both know the truth, don't we? You want to see the world? To do that, you've got to get out there and live in it.' With that, the two men turned their horses toward the rising sun and started a journey with a lifetime of possibilities."

Eugene closed the book and looked around to see who was still awake. Marius was the only one still with him.

"Do you think Flynn will ever go back to Scotia to visit?" Marius asked with a yawn.

Eugene scooped the kid up and deposited him in his bunk bed. "Of course he will." He looked at the ladder to the loft. As planned, Arnie had already disappeared. Eugene pulled the covers up around Marius. "Good-byes don't have to be forever. If people are meant to see each other again, I think they will."

"I like that," Marius mumbled as he rolled onto his side. "Good night, Eugene."

Eugene ruffled his hair one last time. "Night, kid." He waited a bit for the snores and heavy breathing that indicated the rest had gone to sleep. Then he grabbed his bag of possessions — the coveted hair tonic he'd once traded his boots for (that had been fun — trying to explain to Miss Clare why he had no shoes); his trusty comb; his Flynn Rider books; and, of course, his letter, which he had stealthily taken from Miss Clare's office while everyone was at dinner. He climbed up to the loft where Arnie was waiting with the roof hatch already open.

"Ready to do this?" Arnie asked, sounding a bit unsure.

"I was born ready." Eugene hoisted his sack up higher on his shoulder. "Let's go see the world!"

"Shhh!" Arnie looked over the side of the loft. "You'll wake them up."

Below, Eugene could hear Leif wheezing in his sleep.

"Sorry. I'm just excited! Our future starts now."

"Hopefully." Arnie scratched his left eyebrow again.

"Are you having second thoughts?" Now he felt bad. He'd convinced his best friend to leave the only home they'd ever known and join a new crew. Plus, he hadn't told Arnie about the Man with the Mark yet, and he wasn't sure why.

The way Arnie was looking around the loft, he could tell his friend wasn't exactly ready to leave the orphanage behind, and in truth, he wasn't either. But that tattoo . . . he couldn't stop thinking about the man's tattoo. What if it could lead to his parents?

Arnie glanced back at Eugene. "It's just . . . I'm going to miss this place."

Eugene's shoulders sank. The reality was he'd miss it, too. "Same."

"I just didn't think we were leaving *today*, you know?" Arnie started to pace. "We've got a good thing here, and Miss Clare has looked out for us for a long time. I don't want her getting upset when she realizes we're gone."

"True . . ." Eugene started. "But when we drop her a line and send her some money, she'll realize we're okay, and the orphanage will be saved. Think of it as a Lance Archer move."

Arnie brightened. "That's true! We'll save this place from Kurtis Frost. And we get to leave together." He put his arm on Eugene's shoulder and suddenly looked a bit emotional. "Like we always wanted."

Now Eugene was going to get misty. He felt his heart vibrating like a drum. Something told him once he left this room, he'd be charting a course that would change his whole life.

"Together," Eugene said, then clapped Arnie on the back. "So? What are we waiting for? Let's go."

"Okay," Arnie agreed.

Up onto the roof they climbed, then down they rappelled off the side of the building. On the ground, they picked up the lanterns they kept stashed behind the home in case of emergency, and began the walk out of the sleepy village to start their new lives.

"Okay. Where are we headed?" Arnie asked as the village was now in their rear view. "Any clue where the mines are? It's kind of dark out here." Arnie spun around. "There could be spiders anywhere."

"You and the spiders! There are no spiders!" *Of course there are spiders,* Eugene thought. But why alarm his best friend? He held his lantern out in front of him, taking in the vast darkness and wondering where they were headed. He spotted something small and white tacked to a tree in the distance. "Look! There's a sign!"

Below a WANTED poster for Lance Archer was a small, handwritten sign with directions to the village behind them, the kingdom straight ahead, and the Selvag Mines to the left. *Bingo!*

"Left we go!" Eugene said, leading the way.

They walked for what felt like hours, the moon slowly moving along with them, guiding the way. There wasn't a wagon on the road or anyone else foolish enough to head out under the cloak of darkness to find a circus camp. Just when Eugene was ready to admit defeat, he saw a small blaze in the distance.

"Is that it?" Arnie asked. "There's a lot of wagons out there by the mountains."

A caravan was nestled in a half-circle against the entrance to the mines. Eugene could hear the sounds of people talking and laughing that carried over to them on the wind.

"That's got to be it," Eugene said. "Let's go!"

Eugene was moving faster now, the outlines of a large group of men and a fire coming into clear view as he approached. They were sitting around a bonfire, the tiny red embers flying into the air, and he saw lots of people wearing fur, leather, and Viking hats. He didn't see Andy or the Man with the Mark anywhere. Before Eugene could get any closer, Arnie pulled him behind a boulder.

"So what's our plan?" Arnie whispered.

"Our plan?" Eugene questioned.

Arnie peered over the boulder. "Some of those guys look a bit scary. What are we supposed to do? Just walk over in the middle of the night and say, 'Hey, we're here to join the circus!'?"

Eugene peered over the rock next to him. Okay, Arnie had a point. The crew *did* look a bit intimidating. He swallowed hard. There weren't that many boys their own age in the crowd. Just a lot of adults in fur helmets. Wasn't it hot wearing one of those things? he wondered. The helmet hair must be terrible. "Look! I think that's the Baron," Eugene whispered. "What's he saying?"

It was hard to hear from their location, but he could make out words like "plan" and "treasure."

"Are they going on a treasure hunt?" Arnie asked.

"Shh! I'm trying to listen." Eugene strained to hear.

He heard the words "the kingdom" and "guards," but still couldn't catch full sentences. The Baron pulled out a scroll. MISSING: LOST PRINCESS it said. Below was a picture of the missing baby princess that had been pinned to trees and hung all over the village for years. Every once in a while, a royal guard would come through town and replace the worn scrolls with new ones, but the princess's portrait never changed. She would forever be a cherubic baby with big eyes till the day she was finally found. *If* she were ever found.

"Why would the Baron care about the kingdom's lost princess?" Eugene wondered aloud, turning to look at Arnie.

But Arnie was gone.

Something hard landed on Eugene's head.

"Got him!" someone shouted.

In an instant, the world went dark.

SIX

"WHEN YOU DON'T KNOW WHAT TO SAY,
KEEP TALKING TILL YOU MAKE SENSE."
—FLYNNIGAN RIDER IN *FLYNNIGAN RIDER AND THE HUNT FOR THE RED PEARL*

When Eugene came to, his nose twitched at the pungent smell of . . . *human*. And burlap. He was still in the dark, but he could feel his feet bound together as he swung through the air. Wait. Was he upside down? And where was Arnie?

"We found them spying on us, boss!" he heard a male voice say.

"Dump them in the mines!" someone called out, and there was a loud cheer.

This wasn't good. "WAIT! Spying?" Eugene attempted to laugh and spoke loudly, hoping his voice didn't crack under pressure. "No, no, no! You've got the wrong idea. We were invited here by . . . by . . ." Why couldn't he remember the boy's name? Arnold? Adam? "ANDY! That's it! Andy! Tall kid. Decent hair? He said you were hiring workers for the circus."

"Flynn? Flynn Rider?" he heard a familiar voice say. "Is that you?"

"Andy!" Eugene said, suddenly remembering they had given the boy aliases. "Hey there! Remember how you told my friend — uh — Lance and I to come here and sign up? That's what we're trying to do." He cleared his throat. "Although it's kind of hard to when we're swinging upside down."

"Drop them," someone said, and Eugene felt himself hit the ground hard. He quickly pulled the sack off. A group of less-than-friendly-looking men flanked by a huge guy in a metal mask surrounded them. The Baron stood slightly behind them, his face half-covered in the smoky darkness. Andy stood beside him.

Eugene tried to put some room between himself and the body odor stink by backing up, but he banged right into Arnie. *Arnie!* He was lying next to him, still wearing the sack on his head. Eugene quickly pulled it off and saw that his friend was still passed out. It was up to Eugene to talk their way out of this. Luckily, he liked to talk.

"These were the guys I met in the village I was telling you about," Andy told the Baron. "Flynn Rider and Lance . . . What's your friend's last name?"

Last name . . . Eugene thought fast. They couldn't use Archer. Unlike the Flynn Rider books, which did not seem to be well-known, Lance Archer was famous. These guys would know for sure he and Arnie were lying. Eugene looked around, spotting a guy with huge muscles holding a bow and arrow. "Strongbow. His name is Lance Strongbow." He hoped Arnie would approve of his new moniker.

Clink. Eugene turned around and saw the man with a hook for a hand hitting it against a sword. "If they came to join the circus, why'd I find them hiding behind that rock over there while the boss was talking? They were spying!"

"Yeah!" replied a chorus of other unhappy voices.

"No, you've got it all wrong. We were looking for Andy so we could have him introduce us properly! We're two very honest orphans . . . just looking for a place to call home," Eugene added, attempting to gain some sympathy.

"Yeah, right."

He noticed the girl from the ticket booth step forward. Staylan's hair was in braids, and she wore purple breeches and a fitted corset top. She was the only girl he'd ever met who wore pants. "You two? Honest? You tried to scam me into giving you free tickets."

A few of the men drew closer, and Eugene nudged Arnie with his foot, hoping to wake him. No such luck. "Scam? No, no. I wouldn't say scam. There's nothing wrong with asking, though, is there? Guys? Fellas? Any reason you're getting so close?" Eugene started to back up, then noticed the bonfire was only a few feet away. He tried to pull Arnie closer to him, but he was a big kid. Arnie let out a loud snore.

"To the mines!" he heard someone shout, and the men continued to close in.

"Stop!"

They all looked up. The Baron had approached. It was the first time Eugene had gotten a real good look at him. He had the smallest pupils he'd ever seen. His hair, however, looked as good as it had at midday. And in this humidity, too. It was impressive. He wondered how his hair would look like that — all long and flowy.

The Baron smiled at Eugene. "So . . . why do you want to join our crew?"

Eugene thought fast. "To see the world, make money, find treasure." The Baron's eyes widened, and Eugene realized his mistake. "Not that I know there is treasure out there in the world to find, but if there is, I would be happy to get my hands on some."

"I told you they were spying!" a guy shouted, and others started cheering. "They heard you making your next plan!"

"Plan?" Eugene felt himself starting to sweat. "What plan?"

The guy with the hook for a hand bared his teeth. "No one interrupts the Baron when he's percolating a plan!"

"Mines! Mines! Mines!"

Eugene looked at Andy, who just shrugged. Some help he was. Eugene looked at Staylan, who shook her head, whispered something to the Baron, and disappeared into the crowd again. *Wake up, Arnie*, Eugene willed his friend, nudging him again. *Wake up!*

"Silence!" the Baron said. He shot a look at Eugene. "You two stay here while I decide what to do. Men, conference, if you please." The others huddled around him.

Eugene craned his neck to try to hear what they were saying and heard a loud snort. Arnie sat up fast.

"What? Where? What's going on?" he asked.

"Welcome back, *Lance*," Eugene said. "Let me catch you up: Those scary-looking men over there think we're spies and are currently deciding whether to toss us into the mines or to kill us."

Arnie shook his head. "Wha-aat? Did you just call me Lance?"

"Lance Strongbow, actually. And I'm Flynn Rider. You're welcome."

Arnie's eyes widened with recognition, and he scooted closer to Eugene. "So glad you wanted us to leave our home and join the circus, *Flynn*."

"I still think it's a good idea." Eugene watched the men conferring. "They're just a guarded crew. Can't blame them. Shows they're tight-knit and very family oriented, right?" Arnie just looked at him. "Right. Okay, so I guess it's time to come up with a game plan of our own in case they aren't looking to add to their family. How are we getting out of this?"

Arnie thought for a moment. "I say we make ourselves invaluable. Weren't they talking about a treasure before? What if we can find it for them?"

"One problem," Eugene said calmly. "We don't know what the treasure is or if they're actually even looking for some."

"You got a better idea?"

Suddenly a cheer rose up and the men turned around. They didn't look happy.

Eugene looked at Andy.

Sorry, he mouthed.

The guy in the metal mask and the one with the hook hand rushed toward them, followed closely by the redheaded twins. Eugene glanced at Arnie, the heat of the bonfire on their necks. *Plan. He needed a plan!* But before he could think of one, the twin with the sideburns grabbed his arms while the one with the eye patch grabbed Arnie's.

"Apologies, boys," the Baron said as he moved forward. "We've had some issues lately with traitors. And I can't be too careful."

"Hurry up," Sideburns grunted to his partner. "The sooner we get rid of them, the sooner we can get the key."

The key. Eugene decided to take that nugget and run with it.

"We'll get the key for you!" he shouted, and Sideburns dropped his arms in surprise.

The Baron was now looking at him curiously, too.

"That's what you need, right?" Eugene said, his heart thumping hard. "A key to your, uh, treasure? For your, uh, plan? Why don't you let Lance and I get it for you and show we're circus material?" *Circus material? Where was he getting this stuff?*

Arnie thankfully knew exactly where he was going with this. "Yeah. We're quick on our feet, and we know how to get in and out of places unseen. If you need this key, we're the best guys for the job."

Sideburns crossed his arms and scowled. "The Baron told *us* to get the key."

"Yeah, but who would you rather have sweet-talk someone into giving you a key?" Eugene looked at the Baron. "Patchy and Sideburns here, or two sweet orphans?" A few of the men laughed as the twins glared at him. Eugene kept going. "I thought so. And if we find this key for you, then we get to join the crew." *Instead of being dumped in the mines,* Eugene thought, his heart beating fast as he waited for the Baron to respond.

"What do you say?" Arnie asked the Baron. "Is it a deal?"

The Baron seemed to think for a moment. Then he smiled good-naturedly. "Deal."

"What?" Sideburns roared, his face turning as red as his hair.

"They make a good point!" the Baron explained. "These two really are small and wiry."

As much as Eugene took offense at the wiry part, he wasn't about to interrupt.

"With their innocent-looking faces, they'll be in and out in no time." The Baron looked at Eugene and Arnie again and scratched his chin. "Yes, I think you'll do well."

"So what's next?" Eugene asked, glancing around. "Do we leave now?" A few men started to laugh.

"Oh no, you'll leave at first morning light." The Baron sounded a bit more relaxed now that the decision had been made. "The Stabbington brothers will escort you."

"Why do we have to go with them?" Sideburns complained.

"To keep an eye on our new friends, of course," the Baron said. "Just to make sure things go as planned."

Eugene wrung his hands. "Lance and I can get it done. Where are we headed to for this key?"

Sideburns grinned. "It's a quaint place. You boys will eat like kings."

"Like kings! Yes!" The Baron laughed, and the rest of the crew joined in.

Arnie gave Eugene a look. This job sounded worse by the second. "Does this fine establishment have a name?" Eugene asked casually.

The Baron smiled. "Yes. The Snuggly Duckling."

SEVEN

"THERE'S NO GREATER FEELING THAN KICKING OFF AN
ADVENTURE AT EIGHT IN THE MORNING."

—FLYNNIGAN RIDER IN *FLYNNIGAN RIDER AND THE JOURNEY TO SUNRISE LAGOON*

From then on, the names Eugene Fitzherbert and Arnwaldo Schnitz were discarded like outgrown trousers. At sunrise the next morning, Flynn Rider and Lance Strongbow reported for their first adventure: to get a key.

Flynn knew the quest didn't exactly sound exciting, but he was good at drumming it up in his head.

Flynn Rider and his best friend, Lance Strongbow, set off as the sun was rising over the mountains, journeying to find the lost key of Sunrise Lagoon. Yes, they'd face pirates and a sea creature or two, but nothing could stop Flynn and—

"RIDER! Stop standing around and get on your horse already!" Sideburns snapped. "We have to get going!"

"I'm going, I'm going," Flynn said as he attempted to mount the horse next to Lance's. "Gee, you're really not a morning person, are you?"

Getting on a real horse was a lot harder than the imaginary ones he always rode off on when reenacting his Flynn Rider books. But once he pulled himself up and figured out how to get the horse to actually move, Flynn was in better spirits.

Then he noticed that the Baron was waiting to see them off.

Even in the early morning, the guy's hair was perfectly coifed and flowing gently in the breeze. Good hair made a man look powerful, if you asked Flynn. It made him wonder again what he should do with his own locks. Maybe growing them out a few inches would feel right.

"Good morning, sir!" Flynn called to him, trying to be friendly.

"Morning! I just wanted to wish you luck, boys." The Baron took a bite of a juicy red apple. "I'm rooting for you."

"Thank you, sir," said Lance. "We won't let you down."

"That's good to hear." The Baron took another bite. "Because if you do, well . . . that's the end of the line. The Stabbingtons or the guards — whoever comes first — will do away with you. And don't bother using my name to get out of anything either. I'll deny ever having met you."

Flynn tried not to look rattled. "Gotcha: Don't. Mess. Up."

The Baron shrugged. "A man's reputation is all he has; you understand." He tossed Flynn a small velvet bag that jingled. "Give these coins to Anthony the Weasel. And come back with the key."

Sideburns whistled, and his and Patchy's horses took off.

"Have fun, boys!" the Baron said. "Tell Wes the Pest I said hello!" He hit Flynn's and Lance's horses on their hindquarters, and both took off, following the Stabbies'.

"How is 'Don't mess up or you go to the gallows' the Baron's idea of fun?" Flynn asked Lance.

"I guess it's a test, right?" Lance replied, his hands tight around the reins. "If we want to join this circus and be part of their family, our job is to pass." He looked at Flynn. "What kind of name is Anthony the Weasel, though?"

"The kind of name you give a real trickster," Flynn guessed as they galloped down the road. "At least no one knows who *we* really are."

"I have to admit: I really *feel* like a Lance Strongbow now," Lance said with a grin as the horses picked up speed. "And you don't make a bad Flynn Rider."

Flynn gave a wan smile. He'd never warmed to the name "Eugene," though it felt funny to give up the only name he'd ever known. However, if he was starting a new life, what better name was there than his hero's? If only he could come up with the perfect hero look to suit his new persona. He wasn't sure who this new "Flynn" really was yet, but he would figure it out. "I just hope no one hears the name and remembers the books."

"Those books are ancient," Lance said. "No one knows them but you, me, and the boys."

And my parents, Flynn added silently. He wondered again when he should tell Lance about the Man with the Mark. He didn't want to bring it up when they were in the middle of their initiation, but he couldn't keep avoiding the conversation either. How would Lance react? He tried to push the thoughts aside for the moment. First, he had to get this key and gain the Baron's trust, and then he'd find out what the Man with the Mark might know.

They rode for what felt like hours before they finally stopped at a fork in the road, where the Stabbies were already waiting and swigging from canteens. Flynn was thirsty but felt no desire to take a drink from the twins' supply.

"Would you two hurry up?" Sideburns said as they strode over. "Stop chitchatting and tie up your horses over there. This is the end of the line."

"This is it?" said Lance, looking around. "Where's the Snuggly Duckling?"

"Right down the road," said Sideburns, pointing to his left. "And I'd get moving. You've got a half hour to get in and out."

"What happens after that?" Flynn asked as he attempted to get off his steed.

Sideburns and Patchy exchanged looks. "Nothing but trouble. This is not a family joint. Two kids in a place like the Snuggly Duckling will raise suspicions with the royal guards if you're in there for too long."

Flynn bit his lip. Not a family place? "I'm starting to think this Snuggly Duckling is not so snuggly."

"Or friendly," Lance said with a frown.

Patchy stepped forward. He was a foot taller than Lance, but that didn't mean much. Flynn was taller than Lance, too. (Lance swore he was due for a growth spurt any day now.) Flynn stepped between them and focused on Patchy's one eye that wasn't covered with a patch.

"Patchy thinks you're trying to back out," Sideburns said. "Are you?"

"Not at all," Flynn said quickly. "But if Patchy is so worried, why doesn't he tell us that himself?"

"Patchy has no need for talking," Sideburns said. "I know everything he wants to say, so I say it for him."

"Saving his voice, got it." Flynn looked up at Patchy and nudged Lance safely away. "Whatever works for you two! I'm sure Patchy is just keeping an *eye* out for us. Speaking of which, why do you wear that patch?" Patchy continued glaring at him.

"My brother is not your concern," Sideburns said and gave both boys a shove. "Just get in, give the Weasel the money, grab the key, and get to the meeting point, *heroes*. That's what you want, right?"

Flynn decided he would take the hero compliment even if it wasn't meant as one. "Exactly! I take it the meeting point is here, right?"

Patchy rolled his eye.

"After you've made the switch, pull the lever on the duck-shaped drink tap at the bar," Sideburns explained. "It will open a back passageway through the floor. We'll be waiting at the oak tree where the passage lets out." He shot Patchy a knowing look that Flynn wasn't sure he entirely liked.

"One more question: How do we know which gentleman is actually Anthony the Weasel?" Lance asked.

Patchy started to laugh.

"He'll be wearing a tall black hat and have a shiner on his left eye," Sideburns said.

"Shiner on his left eye?" Lance repeated. "How can you be sure it hasn't healed since the last time you saw the guy?"

"He *always* has a bruised left eye. And he's expecting payment, so he'll be looking for someone out of the ordinary crowd, and that's you two. You got the money?"

Flynn held up the velvet bag the Baron had given them. It didn't feel like there were a lot of coins in it, if there were coins at all. He was starting to get a sinking feeling. But there was a lot riding on this — a chance to save the orphanage, to start a new life of adventures with Lance where they could make their own way. Not to mention more potential clues about his parents. "What is this key for, anyway?"

Sideburns grinned, revealing a gold tooth. "You make the crew, you'll find out soon enough. Stop jabbering already and go! You're wasting time."

Flynn and Lance looked at each other. "Want us to bring you back a sandwich?" Flynn asked, and Patchy started to growl. "Okay. Okay. We're going." He turned around and followed Lance. "So what do you think?"

"I think this might be a trap," Lance admitted.

"Yeah, me too. But the Baron needs that key for his plan, so if we can get the key to him and avoid the Stabbingtons, we'll be okay."

Lance kicked up dust with his boots. "Maybe the Stabbies just don't want to see us get all the glory. We'll just have to watch our backs."

Flynn looked. The Stabbingtons were still watching them. "And fronts. Where is this place already?"

All Flynn saw were trees, sky, birds, a few more WANTED posters for Lance Archer, and MISSING posters about the lost princess. Finally, the path dipped down and they rounded a bend.

"Wait! I see something!" He spotted a hand-carved wooden signpost with a wooden duck on it. When he looked up again, he spotted the cottage straight ahead. His stomach dropped.

Lance came running up behind him. "What's it look like? Is it snuggly?"

"It's definitely not snuggly," Flynn said slowly. "If anything, it's crooked."

The establishment was built into the side of a massive tree, seemingly squished under the weight of the twisting, curving branches that wrapped around it, looking anything but structurally sound. A plume of smoke rose from the chimney, proving that there were people inside.

"That's the restaurant?" Lance sounded disappointed. "It looks like a dump. I bet they don't even have food."

They heard boisterous laughter from inside, followed by the sound of yelling and something crashing to the ground. Then someone started singing off-key.

"How many thieves and ruffians do you think are in there, anyway?" Lance sounded nervous.

Flynn swallowed hard. "Too many?" He took a deep breath. "It will be fine. We just need to blend in. Find the Weasel, make the trade, and get to that back exit." There was another crash.

"Back exit," Lance repeated, and his voice squeaked. "Got it. We can do this. But if you want to go first, that's fine by me."

"Oh no, I couldn't." Flynn held his arm out gallantly. "You lead the way."

Lance stared at him. "We'll go at the same time."

"Deal," Flynn said, and gulped. They headed to the door. The noise got louder as they approached.

You are Flynn Rider, he told himself. *You are the most adventurous man alive! You can go anywhere you want!* He pushed open the door. "Garçon? Your finest table . . . please!" His voice petered out. "Oh, hello, gentlemen."

Two dozen patrons dressed in metal and fur, smelling like they hadn't seen a river in several weeks, stopped brawling long enough to stare at the two boys standing awkwardly in the doorway. Somewhere in the distance, Flynn heard a goblet clank to the floor and roll right past them (the floor was just as slanted as the cottage itself). The whole place was lit by dripping candles from two chandeliers and sat on the wood rafters and the crooked balcony. Flynn wrinkled his nose. That was a fire hazard. Another observation: Everyone there seemed to love Viking hats; almost every customer was wearing one, and they were also hung on the walls as decoration.

Flynn looked around, trying to think about what Flynn Rider would do if he were outnumbered and suddenly attacked. In a pinch he could steal one of the axes that hung on the wall next to a mounted deer head. Or maybe he could use one of the arrows embedded in the large practice target in the center of the room.

No one spoke. No one moved. No one invited them in. A few men actually smiled, but the sight was so scary it could have curdled dairy.

Flynn motioned ever so slightly to Lance, and both boys took a step inside.

A man holding a dishrag and a silver mug came out from behind the bar, growling and barreling toward the door. "We don't serve children!"

"Bu . . . bu . . . bu . . . we're not kids," said Lance, tripping over his words. "We're . . . here . . . to . . . Flynn?"

"Yes. We. He. I. We're. I mean, we are here to . . ." Flynn couldn't think of the name. *Is it hot in here?* he wondered. *Definitely stuffy.* His vision swam with weapons and angry scowls, and the awful body odor made him light-headed. "We're here to see someone." *Finally, words!* "Yes! See someone!"

The large Viking put down the silver stein he was polishing and picked each boy up in one of his meaty hands.

"Not this again," Flynn mumbled.

Then he hung them by the backs of their shirts on a set of antlers mounted by the door.

"Gunnar!" someone in the crowd called out. "Anthony is expecting someone, remember?"

"Yes! Anthony, that's it!" Flynn said, filling with relief. "Anthony, the, uh . . ." Was he supposed to use his nickname? "Mr. Anthony Weasel?"

The room burst into laughter.

Gunnar did not laugh. He grabbed the two boys off the antlers and exhaled. The smell of his breath made Flynn nearly pass out. "He ain't expecting kids!"

"The Baron sent us," Lance said.

The room drew in a collective breath.

Gunnar dropped them to the floor as if they were on fire. Two men started sharpening their knives. A third burst into tears. Two others jumped out a window.

"The Baron?" said a man with long white hair who was only wearing underwear. "The Baron himself?" Lance and Flynn nodded. "Why didn't you say so? Go. Do whatever he asked you to do, but make it quick. The guards have already been by here twice today!"

"Helmet!" Gunnar pointed to a small, skinny teen sitting on an even smaller bench in the corner of the room. Gunnar threw an ax across the room, and it struck the wood right above his head. "Play something as a distraction. We don't want the guards sniffing around and digging into things while the Baron is doing his business."

Helmet began playing off-key, and the rest of the men started righting tables, overturning chairs, and picking up the massive mugs that littered the floor.

Gunnar nodded to the bar, where a tall, thin man in a pointy black hat was sitting almost entirely cloaked in shadows with his back turned toward them. "That's the Weasel, right there. Make it snappy if you want to leave here with your life."

"Leaving with our lives sounds good," Flynn said, still unsure what was happening. Were these pub thugs nervous about the Baron or the guards? He didn't want to wait around to find out. He and Lance approached the Weasel slowly while everyone in the Snuggly Duckling watched.

Lance cleared his throat. "Mr. Weasel? We're here to — "

"The Baron sent you?" His voice was barely audible over the sound of the pub thugs pulling their chairs closer to hear the conversation.

"Yes," said Lance, eyeing Flynn. "We work for him."

The Weasel slowly turned around, and Flynn held in his gasp. The Weasel's left eye was black-and-blue and bruised shut as promised. He had a long, pale, narrow face, furrowed eyebrows, and chipmunk-like front teeth. His lips were curved downward in what appeared to be a permanent scowl as he looked from one boy to the other. "He sent children to do a job as important as this one?"

"We're older than we look," Lance tried, but the Weasel wasn't having it.

"I'm insulted," the Weasel huffed. "But I'll be less so if you have what I asked for."

Flynn pulled the velvet bag out of his pocket and held it up as proof. The Weasel's eye widened. Then Flynn quickly put the money back in his pocket before someone tried to poach it. "You have the key?"

"Not so fast, boy." His eye narrowed. "If you're really the Baron's men, you'll be able to answer this question: What does the Baron call me?"

The boys looked at each other, stumped. Flynn rattled his brain for the answer. "The Baron didn't say there would be a quiz."

The Weasel leaned back and watched them. "All men who work with the Baron know the answer. A fake name and reputation is all a man has."

"Don't we know it," said Lance, laughing nervously.

The Weasel didn't laugh along with him. "I'm waiting."

The door to the Snuggly Duckling opened suddenly, and a man in a Viking hat slammed the door behind him. "The guards are on the way back for another check!"

Flynn's heart started to beat fast. They were running out of time. If they didn't get that key, they wouldn't be working with the Baron, and if they didn't work with the Baron, he'd never learn what the Man with the Mark might know about his parents.

"Guess we won't be doing business today, boys," said the Weasel, his speech lingering on the word "boys." He started to rise from his seat.

Flynn didn't want to be considered a boy or a joke. *What would Flynn Rider do in this situation?* he wondered. The Baron *had* to have told them something. *Think like Flynn, Eugene!*

The Weasel started to walk away.

What had the Baron said? He talked about the key, the money, and said . . . "Wes the Pest!" Flynn blurted out, and the Weasel stopped and turned around. "He said to send his regards to Wes the Pest." Weasel sort of growled. "He said it with lots of love. I could tell."

"Me too," Lance chimed in.

He was sweating so bad, it looked like he had been caught in the rain. Flynn was certain he didn't look much better.

The Weasel smiled thinly and walked back over to them as the rest of the Snuggly Duckling watched. Someone fell off their chair, and there was another loud clang. "Let's trade."

"Yes, sir." Flynn placed the money bag on the counter. "Now your turn."

"Guards are nearing the door!" Helmet whisper-shouted.

The Weasel placed a hand in his pocket and pulled out an old key. He placed it in Flynn's hand. The key was small but heavy, with a comblike edge and a decorative scalloped handle with a golden sunburst.

"Better get going if you actually expect to deliver that to the Baron," the Weasel said, placing the money bag inside a leather pouch at his side. "And tell him if he needs help with his latest plan, I'm always up for an adventure." Then he skulked into the shadows and out of sight.

Latest plan? No matter. First part of our mission is complete! Flynn thought.

"They're here!" Helmet cried.

Thinking fast, Flynn grabbed a fork wrapped in a napkin from the table. He slipped the key inside the napkin with the fork for safekeeping and put it in his pocket.

"Flynn! We've got to go!" Lance hissed. His eyes landed on the wooden duck on the tap behind the bar. He scrambled over to it and pulled it back with one strong, swift motion.

There was a clicking sound, and the two of them watched in awe as some of the wooden planks in the floor opened, revealing stairs that led downward. At least the Stabbington brothers had been telling the truth about that.

Lance grabbed a lantern on the counter and started down the stairs. "Flynn! Come on!"

Flynn patted his pocket reassuringly to feel for the key and started for the passageway. The door to the Snuggly Duckling burst open. Three guards stood in the doorway. Their red uniforms had gold chest plates adorned with the same sunburst that was on their helmets. The guard in the middle's helmet had gold feathers, while the others had red. Flynn had to assume he was the captain of the royal guard.

He locked eyes with Flynn. "You! Stop right there!"

Flynn did the opposite. He raced down the stairs before the captain could even cross the dining room. As Flynn's boots reached the bottom step, Lance hit a lever and the stairs disappeared.

"Safe!" Lance said with glee. "You got the key, right? Show me!"

"Here it is!" Flynn's heart was still beating wildly as he took the napkin out of his pocket and unwrapped the key. The pair looked at it, and Flynn shoved the fork in his other pocket. He didn't need the fork, but it might come in handy as a weapon. Did he need a weapon? Above them, they could hear the heavy footsteps of many feet and lots of shouting.

Lance shuddered. "Come on. Let's move." He held the lantern up into the darkness. "I'm not going to think about how many spiders are down here."

"I'll protect you, buddy." Flynn put the key in his pocket again. If they didn't have the lantern Lance had grabbed, they'd be entirely in the dark. Now he could see they were in some sort of underground cave. Other than a few barrels stored in crevices among the natural rock walls, there was nothing to see but the path. They moved quickly. They could still hear shouting above them.

"Let's just follow this path and hope it leads us back up to the tree where we'll meet the Stabbington brothers — AAH!" Lance jumped. Straight ahead, the lantern washed a glow over a skeleton with a sword through its chest. Lance carefully stepped around it. "I do not want that to be *future me*."

"It's not a good look for either of us," Flynn agreed, sliding past the skeleton and picking up his pace.

Behind them they could hear the sound of loud banging and then what could only be described as splintering wood.

The captain's voice rang out loud and clear. "Down here! There's a path!"

Flynn and Lance looked at each other in alarm.

"Stop right where you are!" the captain shouted.

"Go! Go! Go!" Flynn cried as the two ran into the darkness, not stopping till they reached a fork in the path. Both sides looked identical.

"Where do we go?" Flynn asked, his voice echoing. When he really squinted into the darkness, the left path did look slightly brighter. Did that mean it led to daylight?

"They went this way!" the guards shouted, and Flynn could hear them getting closer.

"Go left!" Lance cried. He grabbed a barrel that was lined up along the wall and rolled it back toward the guards. Then he tore off down the path, and Flynn followed, the lantern jumping and making shadows on the darkened walls.

After what felt like an eternity, he heard Lance shout. "I see light! Look!" His friend pointed to a small carving of a tree on the wall and an arrow pointing upward. Lance swung the light onto the short path, which was on an incline that led to a ladder. At the top, Flynn could see a hatch.

"That has to be it!" Flynn said. "Go!" *We're going to make it!* he thought as Lance began the climb first.

"They went this way!" he heard the captain shout.

Or not.

He hurried up the ladder after Lance, feeling like he was going to throw up.

Lance pushed on the hatch. "It won't open!"

"Let me try." Lance dropped back down a few rungs, and Flynn threw his shoulder against the hatch. It still wouldn't budge. "Maybe if we both try!"

They pushed in unison, and finally the hatch burst open, bathing the cave in more light. Flynn tried to pull himself up, but the narrow hatch was tight, and roots had grown over the opening.

"What's up there? Is that a way out?" Lance called up to him.

Flynn could only get his head and chest out; it looked like they were inside a hollow tree. He yanked on a few roots and pulled himself out further. The Stabbingtons were standing there, watching him struggle.

"Help me up!" Flynn called to them.

"You have the key?" said Sideburns flatly.

"Yes, but guards are on our tail!" Flynn said. "Help us out of this thing."

He felt Lance push him from below. "Flynn! Hurry! They're coming!"

Sideburns didn't move. "Show me the key first."

"What? I don't think you understand," Flynn said, still struggling to pull at the roots around him. "We're being chased by royal guards! Get us out first."

Patchy held out his hand, and Sideburns smiled. "Key," said Sideburns. "Or we leave you to rot."

Flynn thought for half a second. He needed help, and the Stabbies were huge. Those brutes could easily yank out the roots with one tug. "Fine," he said with a sigh as he struggled to put his arm down at his side and pull the napkin out of his pocket. He lifted his arm up again and handed them the napkin. "Here. Now help us out."

"Flynn!" Lance shouted.

Sideburns took the napkin and placed it in his vest pocket. He whistled for his horse.

Flynn's heart sunk. He knew what was about to happen. "Wait!" He squirmed and struggled to pull himself out, but it was no use. "Wait!" Sideburns and Patchy ignored him. All Flynn could do was watch as Patchy climbed onto his own horse.

"See you, kid!" said Sideburns as the brothers laughed and galloped away.

EIGHT

"STICKY SITUATIONS CALL FOR STICKY SOLUTIONS."

—FLYNNIGAN RIDER IN *FLYNNIGAN RIDER AND THE HUNT FOR THE RED PEARL*

Flynn groaned in frustration. "Cheats!"

"Flynn!" Lance's muffled voice echoed up to him, and he felt him pushing on his boots from inside the tunnel. "What's going on? The guards are coming! Are the Stabbingtons up there or not?"

Not. They'd have to do this without them. Flynn scanned the area for something that could help them get out of this sticky situation. If only he had something sticky. Or a solution. The distant sound of a neigh caught his attention. The Stabbies may have ditched them, but his and Lance's horses were still out there. That was good! If he could get him and Lance out of this tree trunk, they'd have an escape plan.

"Flynn!" Lance pushed harder. "Let's go!"

Flynn gritted his teeth and looked at the numerous roots still blocking their exit. He reached up and grabbed one of the rocks wedged into the opening, then used it to begin stabbing at the roots, cutting them loose one by one.

"Flynn!" Lance shouted again. "They're coming!"

"Working as fast as I can!" Flynn shouted. The more vines and roots Flynn cut away, the easier it was for his chest to push through the opening, then his torso. Slice, slice, slice. He put down the rock and began to pull himself through, grunting and groaning the whole way till he was clear. "YES!" Flynn shouted to the sky.

"Stop cheering and get me out of here!" Lance said as his head, shoulders, and right hand emerged from the ground. Lance looked around in surprise. "Where are the Stab — AAAH!" Something — a guard, presumably — yanked Lance down from below.

Flynn dove over and reached for Lance's hand, holding on tight. It felt like he was back at Miss Clare's Home for Boys, participating in a famous tug-of-war session.

"Don't let go!" Lance cried.

"I'm not!" With a fierce yank, Flynn pulled Lance's torso clear. Lance kicked out of the guard's grasp and scrambled out of the hole. The two took deep, gulping breaths, their chests rising and falling fast as they stared at each other. "Well, that was fun," Flynn said.

They heard a squeak and turned around. A hand was coming out of the hole.

"Oh no, you don't!" Lance dove for the hole and pushed the hatch down hard, the hand narrowly making it back inside.

"Oww!" they heard someone scream.

Flynn winced. "Sorry!" he yelled and dropped a rotted tree log on top of the hatch to hold it closed. He and Lance high-fived.

"Let me guess: The Stabbies are backstabbers?" Lance asked, still breathing heavily.

"You win a gold coin!" Flynn said. "Let's get back to the Baron." They started running down the path toward the horses.

"But we don't have the key!" Lance cried. "Didn't you just give it to Sideburns and Patchy? We can't go back to the Baron empty-handed."

Flynn grinned. "Oh, but we won't." With a smile and a flourish, he pulled the napkin out of his pocket and unwrapped it, revealing the key inside.

Lance's jaw dropped. "How did you . . . ?"

"Just a little switcheroo with a second napkin and a fork," he bragged. "Now we just have to beat those backstabbers back to the Baron without getting — "

There was a loud boom, and the boys looked back at the tree just as the hatch door blew off. The captain's gold-feathered headpiece began to emerge.

Lance and Flynn didn't waste time. They ran and practically threw themselves into the saddles.

"Go, horse! Go!" Flynn instructed as several guards emerged. His horse didn't budge.

"Flynn, try this." Lance squeezed his legs, then gave the horse a kick in the flanks. The horse took off like a shot.

Flynn did the same, and his horse followed Lance's, galloping as if Flynn had always been his trusty rider. The guards were screaming as they kicked dust up in their faces. They were making their getaway! The wind was in his face, and his hair was blowing, making Flynn think he must look kind of cool. It must have been what the real Flynn Rider felt like! "Yes!" Flynn shouted. "What a morning!"

Lance pointed out the horseshoe prints in the mud as they rounded the curve. "By the looks of those hoofprints, the Stabbingtons can't be that far ahead."

"Maybe we can catch them!"

Up ahead, a broken-down wagon sat in the middle of the road as a man tried to fix a wheel. Barrels of apples ripe for the picking sat in the back of the wagon, and Flynn was reminded yet again how hungry he was. He never had gotten that five-star meal at the Snuggly Duckling the Baron had promised.

"There they are!" the captain shouted.

Flynn did a double take. The guards were barreling toward them at a speed much faster than the two of them were going as novice horsemen.

"Take a left!" Lance said and pulled tight on the reins. His horse made a sudden turn, leaping over a small pile of rocks and making his own path through the brush and trees.

"How did you do that?" Flynn yelled, but Lance was already sprinting ahead. "I can do this. I can do this," Flynn told himself as he squeezed his leg against the horse's left girth, hoping the motion had the right effect. The horse sprang into action, and Flynn whooped loudly. He turned into the trees and tried to keep up with Lance's horse. He looked back and didn't see any sign of guards. "I think we — Pfft! Pfft! I think I swallowed a bug." He stopped short and started coughing.

Lance stopped. "You can't keep your mouth open while you're riding! Even I learned that by now." He hit Flynn on the back, and Flynn stopped coughing. "But if you were about to say we lost them, I think you're right."

Flynn cleared his throat and listened to something in the distance. "Hey. Do you hear that trickling sound? Is that water?"

Both boys dismounted and looked around the wooded area. Flynn didn't see a stream or a river anywhere. Tired, he leaned on the flower-covered rock beside him, and his hand went right through. "What in the name . . ." He ducked his head underneath the vines. Lance did the same. Both boys stared at the cave in front of them.

"I don't like the look of this," said Lance. "It's creepy."

"Creepy, yes, but it could lead to another path back to the circus," said Flynn, stepping inside. "If we go back the way we came, the guards will be waiting for us. Let's just see where this goes." He could see light up ahead, so he knew the cave wasn't that big. He kept walking, and the sound of water grew louder.

"What if I don't want to know where this cave goes?" Lance whispered. "What if you're leading us right into the mouth of a giant spider that eats children?"

"Spiders don't eat people," Flynn said. "They eat . . . other bugs — I think — and . . . What is that?" He exited the cave and looked up.

In the distance stood a single vine-covered ivory tower at the base of a waterfall. Flynn blinked twice, wondering if it was a mirage. Was it abandoned, or did someone live there? Who would live in a lone tower in the middle of the woods, cut off from the rest of civilization?

"You think someone is actually inside that thing?" Lance wondered aloud, reading Flynn's thoughts. "Maybe we could hide out in there."

Flynn stared at the tower. From this distance, he could see no entrance, no doors, no stairs. Just a single window high up near the top, and the shutters appeared to be closed tight. It looked like a good hiding spot. But how would they even get up there? Or get down? They'd have to somehow climb the tower, and neither of them had anything to climb with.

"Looks like too much work to get in," Flynn said reluctantly. "Besides, we have to get back to the Baron before the Stabbies do."

"Good point. And it looks like there is no other way out of this cavern. If the guards find us here, we're done for." Lance turned back to the cave. "Let's go."

Flynn took one last look at the tower, then they both reentered the cave and headed back to the entrance. "The guards are probably way past us at this point anyway."

They got back on their horses — it was easier to mount the horse this time around — and headed back to the road. All appeared quiet.

"I think we're in the clear," Lance said at the same time someone shouted, "There they are!"

Flynn looked up in surprise. Two guards were galloping straight toward them. "What'd they do? Take a lunch break?"

Flynn squeezed the horse's flanks to make him take off like an arrow, but it still wasn't fast enough. The guards were gaining on them, and the broken-down wagon was still blocking the road. The man had even unloaded his apple barrels now. There was no way to get around him.

Whish! Flynn felt something brush his leg.

"I've got them!" said one of the guards as he pulled up alongside them.

Flynn kicked his horse to move faster and pulled away again, catching up with Lance. "What do we do?"

Lance pursed his lips, then his eyes lit up. "Apple pie!"

Flynn's eyes widened with recognition. "Lance Strongbow, you are brilliant!"

Lance winked. "I know."

They rode faster now, pulling away from the guard and riding in tandem till they reached the two apple barrels.

"Watch out!" the man shouted as Flynn's foot flew through the air and hit the first barrel at the same time Lance's did the same with the second barrel.

Both barrels flipped, and apples bumped and rolled down the road behind them in all directions, causing the first guard to stop short. His quick stop caused him to pitch forward over the reins and collide with the wagon owner. The captain came upon the scene seconds later, and his spooked horse took one look at the commotion and turned the other way.

"Sorry!" Flynn called out as they raced away.

Even from a distance, Flynn could hear a lot of shouting. He looked back and made eye contact with the captain.

"You won't get away with this!" the captain yelled.

"I think we already have!" Flynn shouted as he and Lance tore down the road.

They didn't stop till they made it back to the circus. Flynn was just about to say they were in the clear when he saw a barrel flying toward them.

"Duck!" he shouted as the barrel whizzed past their heads.

"Flynn! Lance!" Andy came running toward them, his eyes wide. "You guys came back!"

"Why wouldn't we?" Flynn asked, dismounting with a bit of style this time around.

Andy wiped his brow. "Because you didn't get the key. The Stabbington brothers told the Baron you tricked them and ran off."

"*We* tricked *them*?" Lance asked. "Sorry, but I think it's the other way around."

Andy looked confused but didn't get a chance to say another word before they heard the Baron shouting at the Stabbies.

". . . I trusted you two, and you bring me back a fork?"

Flynn and Lance looked at each other and smiled.

"Shall we go explain what happened?" Flynn asked calmly.

Lance grinned. "With pleasure."

"I don't get it," Andy said, following along behind them.

"You will soon, Andy," Flynn said.

They made their way to the bonfire, where the Stabbingtons were still getting reprimanded.

"Looking for this?" Flynn interrupted. He pulled the gold key out of his pocket and held it high in the air.

The Baron's jaw dropped. "How did you . . . ?"

"Oh, we just did what you told us to do," Flynn said, eying Sideburns and Patchy.

"But . . . You . . . We . . ." Sideburns stuttered.

"Lance and I learned a long time ago that the only backup we need is each other," Flynn explained. "No hard feelings, fellas." The Stabbies grimaced.

The Baron crossed his arms. "What happened out there?"

"These two" — Lance pointed to the brothers — "took what they thought was the key, then ran off instead of helping us out of a jam with the guards."

"Boss, they were so slow they were going to get us caught," Sideburns explained. "We had to leave them behind."

"With the key?" The Baron glared at the brothers, then turned his attention back to Flynn. "Do the guards know what you were after?"

"No!" Flynn said quickly. "All they know is that two kids were in the Snuggly Duckling and that we tried to escape, but they have no clue why. The Weasel disappeared before we did. He said to tell you if you want help with your plan, he's in." He put the key in the Baron's hand.

The Baron snorted. "Of course he wants in. Anything else?"

"The guards can't be far behind," Flynn added. "You might want to hide this somewhere before they show up."

The Baron stared at Flynn and Lance for a moment, then looked at the Stabbingtons. "You two are on manure duty for the rest of the week!" The brothers groaned. "You're lucky your fate is not worse!" Then he looked back at Flynn and Lance. "And as for you two . . ."

Flynn's whole body stiffened. Had they passed the Baron's test or not?

Finally, the Baron cracked a smile and started to laugh. Flynn and Lance looked nervously at each other before joining in.

The Baron pulled them into a bear hug. "You two are keepers! Welcome to the circus, boys."

"Really?" Lance sounded excited. "We can stay? We're employed?"

"Employed?" the Baron boomed. "You're family now!"

Lance beamed, leaning into the hug.

"And you get paid every Friday," the Baron added. "Of course, there are extra opportunities to make money, but I'll let the crew tell you about those. You're one of us now, and we take care of one another."

"I like the sound of that!" Flynn said.

The Baron turned the boys around to face the crowd. "Everyone, let's welcome the newest members of our family!" The crew started to cheer.

Flynn smiled at Lance. They'd finally started the next chapter of their adventures and found a new place to belong.

He just had to hope their future jobs wouldn't be this hairy.

NINE

Less than twenty-four hours earlier, the crew surrounding Flynn were ready to toss him and Lance into the mines or do much worse.

Now?

Flynn felt himself being lifted up onto the shoulders of the stockiest man in fur he'd ever seen. Flynn grabbed hold of the antlers on the guy's Viking helmet to keep from falling off. To his right, Lance was held in the air by a muscular guy in a metal Viking face mask. Flynn noticed he had a cupcake tattoo on his upper right arm.

"We have the key!" crowed the men, high-fiving and hugging one another.

Flynn couldn't believe people were this excited about a key. As the big guy carted him around on his shoulders, the other circus workers kept patting him and Lance on the back and thanking them for pulling off the heist. The Baron watched it all from the sidelines, looking as pleased as plum pudding.

So was Flynn. He could get used to being the center of attention.

The crew loved them! Well, most of them did. The Stabbington brothers had already skulked off in a huff. But the crew who had been scowling at them the night before were now cheering, and Andy was practically in tears he was so happy. In the light of day, Flynn could see there were dozens in this motley crew, some as young as he and others as old as the Baron. No two people looked alike. Many wore Viking hats and fur, while others wore regular dress adorned with leather vests and high boots. And then there was the mime in white face paint pretending to blow up balloons. Even Staylan was there. Flynn caught her eye, and she gave him a small nod. The only person he didn't see was the Man with the Mark, but he had to be there somewhere.

When Flynn and Lance were finally placed on the ground again, a crowd gathered around them. Flynn felt like he was floating.

"Nice job!" said a boy in a high-pitched voice with an unusually large sniffer as he pulled Flynn outside of the circle. "I'm Big Nose. I think you and your buddy over there are going to be bunking in the tent I share with Andy."

Andy threw an arm around Flynn. "I'm so glad you survived the test!" he said. "I should have warned you about our initiations. Circuses are not for the faint of heart, and it scares most guys off."

"I wonder why," Flynn said dryly.

Andy laughed. "But I knew you guys could handle it. Welcome aboard! I'm going to go find you two some bedding for our tent. You're going to love it." He high-fived Flynn and ran off.

A shadow fell over him and Big Nose, and they looked up. The guy who had just held Flynn in the air was glaring at him with small, beady eyes. He thrust something small at Flynn, and Flynn caught it. It was a tiny wooden unicorn.

"Vlad is giving you a present," Big Nose explained. "Wow. He never gives his unicorns away for free." Vlad grunted. "He doesn't talk much, but he loves unicorns! He's always carving them and selling them at the circus. He makes decent money with them, too."

"Uh, thanks, Vlad," Flynn said to the massive Viking. Seemingly satisfied, the man turned away.

"The Baron lets us all make and sell things at the circus if we want, but most guys earn better money other ways," Big Nose said. "We'll show you how it's done once you're settled in."

Someone started to sing a song off-key while a few men grabbed lutes.

"Flynn!" Lance came up and put his arms on Flynn's shoulders. "Can you believe this celebration? We're in! We're officially part of the crew now!"

The last time Flynn had seen Lance this happy was the day the whole orphanage went on a field trip to the farm and the owners let him help make supper with the eggs they'd gathered.

"You were so right," Lance said. "This was the right move for us. They've seen every kingdom you can think of as part of the circus! The guy who was carrying me around? Atilla? He even loves to cook, just like I do."

"He makes the best desserts," Big Nose chimed in. "Hi. I'm Big Nose, by the way." He held out his hand and Lance shook it fiercely.

"Nice to meet you, Big Nose," Lance said cheerfully. "Oh, and Flynn, this is Ulf." The mime slid past them, pretending to gallop on a horse. Unlike the other men, Ulf wore red suspenders and a striped T-shirt along with white gloves. The look worked for him.

"Nice Rider impression, Ulf!" Big Nose nudged Flynn in the shoulder. "He's mimicking you, get it? Flynn Rider — that's why he's riding a horse."

"Is it?" Flynn felt like this was a bit of a stretch, but who was he to say? "Thanks, Ulf!"

"You've got to meet the Hook brothers," Big Nose added. "They're great guys, too. Don't let them scare you off. Hook Hand! Come here!"

Two young men wearing fur came walking over. Both had early baldness, one with patches of hair that looked like horns. One was missing a foot, the other a hand, hence their names.

"Let me get this straight: You guys are brothers and you both have hooks for appendages?" Flynn said, and Lance sighed. "Was that not appropriate?"

The bald one's eyebrows creased, giving him the look of someone who mean-mugged for a living. Then he broke into a wide smile. "It's a family thing."

"I'm Hook Foot," said the brother with a hook for, well, his foot. "And my brother goes by Hook Hand on account of, you know . . ."

"Don't you 'you know' me!" Hook Hand growled. "I can do a lot more with one hand than most men can do with two."

"It's true!" Big Nose agreed. "Hook Hand is our resident piano player . . . when we actually have a piano."

"I've broken a few," Hook Hand admitted, "but I always get my hand on a new one. Piano is way more important to the circus than dance."

Hook Foot growled. "Not this again! How many times do I have to tell you? Dance makes guests happy — way happier than hearing someone play the piano!"

Hook Hand got into his brother's face. "Says who?"

"Says me!" said Hook Foot, going nose to nose with his brother.

They started pushing and shoving each other. They could still be heard arguing as they disappeared in the crowd.

"Nice guys," Lance said, giving Flynn a questioning look.

"You'll get used to them," Big Nose said. "They're as loyal as they come. We're one big family here thanks to the Baron. Speaking of which, here comes his daughter, Staylan. She scares me." Big Nose squeaked.

Flynn looked up. He couldn't help taking in Staylan's violet eyes, the mole on her left cheek, and the choker around her neck. She was the only girl his own age Flynn had been around in a while — he had grown up in an all-boys' orphanage, after all — but if it bothered her to be in the minority, she didn't show it. Her face was dead serious as she approached them.

"My dad has a lot of work to do; he wants to see you both," she said flatly. "Like, now."

"Hiiiiii . . . Staylan," Big Nose squeaked.

She barely looked at him. "Hi." She turned and walked away.

Big Nose sighed. "I wish I could talk to people like that. She's amazing."

"FLYNN! LANCE! Let's go!" she shouted. Staylan disappeared into the largest tent in the encampment.

"You two better go," Big Nose said. "It's never good to keep the Baron waiting." Flynn made a face. "Don't worry. If you were in trouble, you'd know it. He probably just wants to show you the ropes." He grinned, revealing a few crooked teeth. "You're going to love it around here. You guys are going to have more money than you ever dreamed!"

Lance nudged Flynn. "You hear that? We're going to have money! And we can send some back to the orphanage! I'm so glad you suggested we join the circus!"

Flynn couldn't help but get a little caught up in it all, too. Their life's adventure — the one they'd dreamed about on the rooftop of Miss Clare's Home for Boys for so long — was finally happening. They were going to see the world with the circus. He knew his parents were out there somewhere. And now he could find them.

"Big Nose! Come on! I need help putting this stuff away!" Vlad yelled. He had a stack of royal-guard chest plates in his arms.

How did he get those? Flynn wondered.

"I have to go, but I'll see you at dinner," Big Nose told them. "I think Atilla is making cupcakes in your honor!"

"Cupcakes? Oh man, I would have helped him bake those," Lance moaned. "Next time, I guess. Let's go find Staylan."

Flynn was quickly learning the campground was a maze. In addition to all the wagons, they seemed to have twice as many tents — some for the circus itself, which were all set up in the performance area, others for the crew who lived and worked there. Many had smaller fires set up in front of their campsite along with wood stumps that doubled as chairs. As they walked, Flynn could see a long laundry line hung between several tents and a group of men in the middle of a heated game of what looked like chess. Reaching the Baron's tent, they ducked inside. Their boss's digs were markedly upscale — beautiful rugs overlapped one another on the floor, and everything was illuminated by lanterns strung across the tent. Two cots overflowing with pillows were in one corner, while an eating area was in another. A group of small potted cacti and several framed paintings of fruit and a river were propped up in each corner. Flynn didn't recognize the artist. Maybe Staylan had painted them?

"There are my stars!" the Baron boomed, seemingly delighted to see them. "Thanks for bringing them to me, Staylan, my love."

"Sure, Daddy." She gave him a kiss on the cheek before shooting Flynn a look that could kill on her way out.

The Baron pointed a finger at Flynn's chest. "I had a good feeling about you two! Come on over and collect a prize."

"A prize?" Lance said, his eyes widening.

"Of course! I told you boys — we're a family, and family takes care of one another." He clapped Lance on the back. "Hard work is rewarded around here. Come with me." The Baron steered them toward a corner of the tent where there were several burlap sacks. He untied them, and Flynn gasped. The bags were overflowing with pearls, necklaces, chunky gold bracelets, and pocket watches along with rings, earrings, and was that a gold parasol? Flynn reached down and touched a gold sunburst medallion on a chain.

"The symbol of the kingdom, I'm told," the Baron said. "I saw that, learned about this beautiful kingdom of yours, and decided we had to visit." He put a hand on Flynn's shoulder. "See anything you like? Think of it as a present."

"No one has ever given me a present before," Lance said, picking up a string of pearls and running it through his fingers. "I mean, at the home, we made each other stuff, but it wasn't anything like this."

"Hey," Flynn scoffed. "You said you liked that papier-mâché mask I made you."

Lance looked baffled. "That was a mask? It had one eyehole."

"Clearly, I'm an abstract artist."

The Baron laughed jovially. "Well, I have no masks, but there are jewels and some leather goods in there. Go ahead — dump them out and look! I want you to pick something that will remind you of your first week in my care." He patted both boys on the back. "I can't wait to show you all the circus has to offer. The things we've seen in our travels . . . it's a life like no other, and the joy we bring to the people, well . . ." The Baron's eyes looked watery. "You'll see. Some of the folks we perform for have never seen a live show before — experienced the magic of a dragon, seen an elephant up close, or an old man turn young again. For a moment, we are able to take them out of their sometimes dreary lives and allow them to imagine something better. It's heroes' work what we're doing."

"Wow," Lance said. "That sounds really nice."

"It does," Flynn agreed. "It's almost as if this circus thing is more than just a circus."

The Baron smiled. "Exactly. It is! Truly! The circus is a way of life and a way to share joy with the kingdoms. We're lucky to do what we do, and I'm thankful to have my family to do it with me."

Flynn beamed. Here was their new boss saying he wanted to show them the ropes when he didn't have to. He could make them toil away as the lowest-ranking members of the crew, but instead, he was giving them a leg up. It only made him admire the Baron more.

"Where'd you get all this stuff, sir?" Flynn picked up a shiny pocket watch and let it swing from its gold chain.

"Now, Flynn, call me the Baron. No more 'sir'!" He picked up a gold cuff bracelet. "As for where I procured these things, people lose stuff all the time at the circus. They're so busy having fun, they don't even notice what they've lost till they're already home, and even then, they can't be sure where they misplaced it."

"You mean you stole it?" Flynn felt his heartbeat start to race. Buying a key in a shifty pub was one thing . . . but outright *thievery*?

The Baron laughed, holding his belly. "Oh, Flynn. You didn't think we did as well as we do for ourselves just selling moonstone tonic and peepholes in a dragon cart, did you?" He put his arm around him. "I'm in charge of a lot of men, and I take that responsibility seriously. I need to look out for you all."

"Like at the orphanage," Lance said slowly. "It was like that there, too."

"Exactly!" The Baron nodded. "I don't want my men going hungry or looking for odd jobs in order to send money home to their mothers. When you work with me, you're guaranteed a job — as long as you do it well, of course. And sometimes you need extra incentives. I make sure all the men are rewarded."

"Ah, well, that's very generous of you," Lance said and looked at Flynn, hesitating. "You're just keeping the lost stuff that people don't come back for. That's not so bad, right?"

"Right," the Baron agreed.

"Oh . . . neat," Flynn said. Like Lance, he still felt a bit uneasy. Call it what you want, but this was still stealing, wasn't it? "Is this why the royal guards were after us this morning — did they think we stole that key?"

"Nah! I'm not sure they even knew that key was missing," the Baron said. "If anything, they chased you down because you were two kids in the Snuggly Duckling, a place you shouldn't be spending time in — unless you're with me! Stick with me boys, and I'll take you places." He nudged them both toward the bags. "Now pick something."

"Okay." Lance fished his hand into the bag and pulled out a gold hoop earring. "Flynn! Look! Doesn't this look like Archer's? I always wanted one just like it, but orphans don't get jewels like this."

"You're not an orphan anymore, Lance." The Baron looked from Lance to Flynn. "What about you?"

Flynn couldn't take his eyes off that bag of jewels. It would be rude to not take something when the Baron was being so generous. He dug into the second sack and noticed a brown leather satchel. He picked it up, taking a whiff of leather. The hide was worn, but not too worn. It had a stitched patch on one side, but it didn't look ratty. If anything, the cracks in the leather gave the bag character. It even had a gold buckle that kept everything secure. If only he'd had this satchel on him when he and Lance were traveling with the key! He'd have had somewhere to put it and wouldn't have had to worry about it flying out of his pocket.

"A fine piece, Flynn," the Baron observed, taking the satchel from his hands and placing it over Flynn's head. "It's yours!"

Flynn took a deep breath and inhaled that wonderful leather smell. He placed the strap over his shoulder and let the satchel hang at his side. It was a little long, but he was growing. Someday it would fit him like a good pair of boots (something else he still needed). But now that he had a job, he could someday buy a pair that fit right. After they sent money to Miss Clare, of course. It sounded like they would have enough money for everything they wanted to do, and then some.

"It suits you!" The Baron took a step back and admired the bag. "Enjoy! I am just so grateful for all you boys did today. That key is going to open a lot of doors for us."

Before Flynn could even ask "what doors," Vlad was racing into the tent.

"Boss! We've got company."

The Baron nodded and turned to Flynn and Lance. "Guards. Boys, let's get you someplace to hide till they're gone."

"Should I bring them to Vedis?" Vlad was already grabbing the sacks of treasures, pulling them closed and throwing them over his shoulder.

"Who's Vedis?" Lance asked.

"A man of few words," the Baron said, "and he usually likes to avoid confrontation at all costs. He usually helps out at the moonstone cart when he isn't training animals."

Flynn's whole body stiffened. *The moonstone cart.* "By any chance, does he have a tattoo on his arm?"

"Most of my men have a tattoo on their arm, Flynn," the Baron said with a laugh. "No, let's not bother Vedis with this," he told Vlad.

"Bother? Who said anything about bothering? Lance and I will be quiet as mice," Flynn said quickly, and Lance looked at him strangely. "Vedis won't even know we're there."

"Boss!" Vlad said. "We've got to go. I already moved the other stuff inside the dragon cart for safekeeping."

"Good. Now where to put these two?" the Baron muttered to himself. He pulled a coin out of his pocket. "We'll let the coin decide — heads the dragon cart or tails with Vedis." He threw the coin into the air.

Flynn held his breath. *Come on, tails!*

The coin landed on its head. "Dragon cart it is." He handed Flynn the coin. "With this coin, heads is always the answer."

Flynn turned the coin over in his hands. Both sides were heads. He looked at the Baron in wonder.

"Another gift from me to you," he said, ushering the boys out of the tent. "Don't lose it. I'm sure it will come in handy someday. Now go and get out of sight."

TEN

"THE WORLD IS MY OYSTER.
GOOD THING I'M NOT ALLERGIC TO SHELLFISH."

—Flynnigan Rider in *Flynnigan Rider and the Secret of Calypso Cove*

Vlad rushed Flynn and Lance over to the dragon wagon and quickly unlocked the chains. "Quick! Get in."

Flynn held his breath. This was it. The moment they'd see exactly what was in that wagon all those people forked over money to peek at.

Vlad pulled open the doors.

Huh?

The only thing in the wagon was a stack of royal guard helmets, the chest plates he'd seen Vlad carrying earlier, some sort of bullhornlike instrument, and paddles.

"What's that for?" Lance asked, pointing to the paddles as he hopped inside.

"It makes our dragon appear." Vlad looked at their blank faces. "You know, you use it to hit the carriage and make it sound like the dragon is moving around. And the bullhorn is for making noises." Vlad ushered Flynn into the carriage. "I'll explain it all after the guards go away. I think you two are on dragon duty this week anyway, so you'll learn soon enough."

"Yes!" Lance said. "That's a good gig, right?"

Vlad snorted. "If you don't mind roasting. It gets hot in this box." He started to lower the tarp over the wagon. "Now just sit quiet and don't touch the other stuff. We will come and tell you when the coast is clear." He dropped the burlap canvas.

"Hey," Lance said as they were shrouded in near total darkness. "What was all that stuff you were asking the Baron about a man with a tattoo?"

Flynn froze. They were alone for the first time since they'd gotten back to camp. Maybe now was the time to tell his best friend about the Man with the Mark! *Vedis.* "Listen, there's something I have to tell you."

"Shh!" Lance whispered. "I think I hear someone coming."

Flynn heard the click of the lock on the chains and tried not to think about how stuffy it was in the wagon already. As his eyes adjusted, he could see some light seeping through the canvas. It was the peephole set up for "dragon" viewing. He and Lance saw it at the same time and dove for the hole, jockeying for position in front of it. The conversation would have to wait.

"What do you see?" Lance hissed, trying to nudge Flynn out of the way.

"Nothing yet," said Flynn.

"Let me look!"

"At nothing?" Flynn planted himself in front of the hole. "Okay, wait. No. I see something now." Three guards were headed their way, including the captain.

"Who is in charge here?" the captain asked as he started striding toward the wagons. Flynn motioned for Lance to be quiet. The captain was uncomfortably close.

"Gentlemen, good morning!" said the Baron, appearing in front of the wagon with the Stabbington brothers. "What can we help you with today?"

"Are you the owner of this circus?" the captain asked.

Flynn moved over so Lance could see through the peephole as well.

"Yes. I am the Great Baron of the Circus of Oddities." The Baron bowed, and Flynn noticed him flick his wrist. The Stabbingtons started to back up toward the guards' horses. "You have heard of me, I assume."

The captain didn't miss a beat. "No."

"Why, surely . . ." The Baron looked shocked. "Oh, well, no matter. I'm sure by this afternoon news of our circus will have spread throughout the kingdom."

"That's why I'm here," the captain said. "While you may have alerted the village to your presence — and several other villages nearby for that matter — you have not gotten permission from the king to perform here."

"That means their showing up here has nothing to do with us," Lance hissed. "That's good!"

Flynn shushed him as the captain looked at the wagon, then back at the Baron.

His brown eyes narrowed. "Performing without consent from the king is considered trespassing."

"Why, we would never! As other kingdoms in the region could tell you, we only come where we are welcome, don't we, crew?"

The Stabbies mumbled in agreement. Flynn watched as Sideburns lingered by the captain's horse while Patchy rubbed its snout. What were those two up to?

"I sent the king a letter with a carrier over two months ago telling him of our arrival and plan to perform for two weeks on this very spot, which, I might add, is not being used for anything since all the mining occurs underground."

The captain stepped closer. "Well, he didn't receive a letter, and we're here to collect the money owed for performing on his land."

"He didn't?" The Baron ran a hand through his hair. "That's impossible! Ulf? When did we send the king that letter?"

The mime shuffled into view and began a series of hand motions that everyone — including the guards — watched with rapt attention.

"Horse," Lance guessed in a whisper, wiping his brow. It was getting very hot in the wagon. "Something about an eight and I think galloping. Maybe?"

"Or the Baron is just stalling for time," Flynn guessed. He looked back at Sideburns again and noticed he was now standing by the saddlebags strapped to the captain's horse, while Patchy waved carrots in front of its snout.

"Captain, I'm so sorry for this mix-up," the Baron said. "I assure you our circus seeks to bring nothing but love and happiness to every kingdom we enter. We never go where we aren't wanted. Crew? Start disbanding the circus. We'll pull up stakes immediately."

"What's he doing?" Lance hissed, but Flynn's eyes were still on Sideburns. He watched as the redhead's knife came down fast, slicing one of the moneybags off the side saddle. Patchy swooped under him and caught it, sliding the bag into his jacket in one swift move while Sideburns offered the horse a carrot with his other hand.

"No need to move on to a new kingdom just yet," Flynn heard the captain say. "If you'd like to stay to perform, you just need to pay the appropriate taxes for land use."

"Of course!" The Baron motioned to Sideburns and Patchy, who left the horse's side and strode over. "Boys? Hand the captain the money we owe."

Sideburns handed the Baron the same small velvet bag that he'd just cut off the captain's saddlebag.

"Please give this to the king with our gratitude for being able to perform for his loyal subjects," the Baron said.

Clever, Flynn thought. Paying taxes to the king with money that had already been collected meant the circus lost nothing. Was that wrong? Maybe. But when it came to taxes, Flynn couldn't help but think of the grief poor Miss Clare and the Home faced with Kurtis. It didn't seem entirely fair for the circus to pay to entertain the citizens on land that wasn't even being used.

"Thank you," the captain said and handed the moneybag off to one of the guards who tied it back to the saddlebag . . . again.

"And please tell him we'd love nothing more than to perform for him personally at your Festival of the Lost Princess," the Baron added.

Flynn had heard about the Festival of the Lost Princess back at the orphanage. This year was the fifth anniversary of the lost princess's disappearance, and the king and queen had planned a celebration in her honor. Miss Clare had said there was even a new reward being announced for anyone who found her. "That reward will make someone as wealthy as the king!" he recalled Miss Clare saying.

Ulf gave the Baron a piece of parchment, which he then handed to the captain. "I have detailed our humble suggestion in this letter. I would be ever so grateful if you'd give it to him, seeing as you're headed back to the castle."

The captain placed the scroll in his saddlebag. "I can do that."

"And you cannot leave without tickets for your families," the Baron added as Ulf handed him an envelope. "Captain, do you have any children?"

"Why, yes," he said in surprise as the Baron handed him tickets. "My daughter Cassandra would probably get a kick out of seeing a real dragon."

"Then you must bring her!" the Baron boomed.

Flynn was sweating, and not just because of the heat in the wagon. Was the captain actually going to fall for this? He tried to suppress the panicked feeling that they were all going to end up in the dungeons.

"I will!" the captain said with a gruff laugh. "I'm looking forward to it, and I'll mention your offer to the king as well. I'm sure he'll be in touch about a festival performance. Good day, Baron."

The Baron bowed. "We look forward to hearing from you all. Please stop by anytime, Captain."

The captain hesitated. "By the way, there was a dustup at the Snuggly Duckling this morning. Two boys, well below the age of their typical customer, ran off when we entered. They wouldn't work for you, would they? We're wondering if they're runaways."

Lance and Flynn both backed away from the peephole.

"The Snuggly what? We're not from here. I'm afraid I've never heard of such an establishment," the Baron said. "Sorry."

"Just wanted to check. Well, then, we'll be off. Good day."

"Good day, Captain!" the Baron said.

He and the other members of the crew waved as the guards mounted their horses and kicked up dust as they tore out. The Baron continued waving until the guards were nothing but a dot in the distance. Flynn felt himself breathe a sigh of relief.

"Sideburns?" the Baron said, his voice low. "You have it?"

"Yeah, boss." Sideburns pulled a second velvet moneybag out of his jacket and tossed it to the Baron.

The Baron opened the bag and counted the coins inside. "Good work. Vlad? Let Flynn and Lance out, please."

Flynn and Lance dove out of the wagon as soon as Vlad rolled up the tarp.

"You weren't kidding about it being hot in there!" Lance said, gulping huge breaths.

"Vlad, did you forget to give them a fan?" Big Nose scolded.

"Sorry!" Vlad said as he locked the dragon wagon back up tight.

Flynn watched the Baron dump the contents of the velvet bag into his palm. There had to be a dozen silver and gold pieces inside. The Baron noticed him watching and looked up.

"You boys look like you could use a drink," he said. "Andy! Can you get them some water?"

"I feel like a dried prune, but no worse for wear," Flynn said.

"Lance!" Andy called to him. "Atilla wants to know if you want to help him make roast duck for dinner!"

"Me, cook a roast? Yes!" Lance grinned at Flynn. "I like circus life already."

He tore off, leaving Flynn with the Baron. "Do you cook, too, Flynn?"

"No, but I am a big fan of eating," Flynn said with a grin as Andy handed him a glass of water.

The Baron laughed. "Me too. So what *is* your skill set?"

"I don't know," Flynn hated to admit. This was the problem. Even now that he had a great new moniker and was in charge of his own destiny, he still wasn't sure who he was. He was pretty decent at acting out stories for the boys, but he didn't know if that was a particular skill. How did a man figure that out anyway? He'd have to keep trying different personas on for size.

"Everyone needs an expertise when they're making their way in the world." The Baron patted Flynn's shoulder. "You'll figure yours out. I know it's hard reinventing yourself at first. It was hard for me, too."

"Really?" The Baron seemed to have it all together.

"Yes. In fact, the first time I was truly hungry, out on my own, I spotted a well-to-do woman with a jade bracelet, and I decided I was going to take it. Oh, it was a beaut! Green jade nestled in a gold strand that hit the sunlight and made you squint. But then I felt bad and second-guessed myself. I wound up not eating for the next six days.

Almost died of starvation." The Baron grimaced. "Meanwhile, she lived like a queen, I'm pretty sure. She had arms full of bangles. She wouldn't have missed that one." He stared off into the distance. "I still regret not taking it. I've never seen a jade bracelet like it since that day."

Flynn listened quietly, unsure what to say. He wasn't even sure the Baron wanted him to chime in anyway.

"The point is, I should have plucked it. She wouldn't have lost anything that affected her, while I would have evened the playing field a bit and had money to find my way in the world. Instead, it took me another year before the heist that . . . well, that's a story for another day." He smiled. "My point is that bracelet has always stuck with me and serves as a reminder that no one looks after you but yourself. I've never wanted Staylan to want for anything. I'm all she has. I've built this circus up to what it is today for her, really. So she'd never have to worry about where her next meal was coming from. And now neither of us wants for anything, and that feels good. And it means we get to keep doing what we love, spreading joy through the circus." His eyes flashed. "Once you get a hold of treasure, you just want more. You'll see."

Would he? "I have never even had a coin to my name."

"Well, you're getting paid now." The Baron smiled. "Your whole life is about to change!"

"You think?" Flynn asked.

"Yes, but what do *you* think?" the Baron countered.

Maybe the Baron was right. Flynn instantly thought of his parents again, and he could see the picture as clear as day. *Flynn Rider rode into a new kingdom with the circus like he'd rode into dozens of others, but this time, a couple was waiting. He looked at them. They looked at him. And Flynn knew for certain these were his parents.*

Flynn grinned. "I think you're right."

ELEVEN

"SO THIS IS WHAT FREEDOM TASTES LIKE—
FRESH AIR, NO RULES, AND NO PROBLEMS."

—FLYNNIGAN RIDER IN *FLYNNIGAN RIDER AND THE JOURNEY TO SUNRISE LAGOON*

I could get used to this, Flynn thought as he woke up well-rested to the sound of birds chattering outside his tent, his roommates snoring, and an elephant trumpeting in the distance. The tent was surprisingly warm, but he liked how it was still thin enough that he could hear men talking on their way to do chores, and smell whatever delicious meal was being cooked up for breakfast.

He knew Lance would make sure it was something good. In the week since they'd arrived, Lance had volunteered for kitchen duty daily, and he was loving it. One morning he made a breakfast quiche, another a hearty beef hash, and everyone was praising his expertise. The Baron (who was especially fond of a good stew) had even started to make requests.

Flynn, on the other hand, had nothing to do till the first circus show started at noon, so when he woke early he'd either go back to sleep or roll over and stare up at the lanterns strung along the tent. There was something about them swaying gently in the breeze that felt very peaceful, like the tent itself. His cot was way more comfortable than his springy mattress back at Miss Clare's Home for Boys, and he didn't have to share a pillow with anyone. He also had a decent blanket that had apparently *fallen off* a wagon passing by the circus just a week before. Everyone had gotten new bedding because of it. (Flynn tried not to ask too many questions and just enjoy his good night's sleep.) Their tent even had a trunk in the corner where they could store their personal effects for travel. He'd tucked his Flynn Rider books in there for safekeeping but kept his new satchel by him at all times . . . not that he had anything to carry in it yet. It just looked good, like something the real Flynn Rider would carry. It made Flynn wonder if maybe the satchel was the key to the whole new look he was trying to achieve.

But there wasn't a lot of time to figure all that out. When the parade first rolled through his village, he hadn't realized how much went into running a circus. Flynn learned a lot of the guys had regular acts: Hook Hand and Hook Foot performed music and dance routines along with mock sword fights during the preshow. Atilla and Vlad handled several animal performances, including a quartet of dancing geese. Ulf put on a mime show during the first act, right after the dancing poodles, while the Baron and Staylan were ringmasters. Staylan also did double duty with the ticket booth. There were acrobats, a choreographed number with horses, along with dazzling sleight-of-hand tricks, and, of course, wagons that became makeshift shoppes, selling everything from sweet treats to the moonstone tonic and the chance to peek inside the dragon cart. No one liked that gig, so the newbies always got it. Flynn had spent the last few days sweating it out inside the cart during performances while also learning the ropes of doing circus "business," as the other guys called it.

"Flynn, the Baron wants me to show you how to sweet-talk a customer today after our second dragon showing," Andy said with a yawn as he started to rise out of bed. "I think it has something to do with what you'll be doing for his next big plan."

Flynn sat up, remembering some vague talk about this plan business. "So these plans, the Baron has one in every kingdom?"

"Yeah." Big Nose was making his bed, tucking the corners of his blanket in so tight, you could bounce a pebble off them. He watched as the boy pulled out a small velvet bag and emptied it into his hands. It was full of coins. Big Nose counted them quickly, then placed them all back in the bag.

Flynn watched him counting with slight envy. He couldn't wait to be working long enough to have money like that. He'd be able to send money to Miss Clare all the time!

Big Nose slipped the velvet bag into his pocket. "We all have roles to play, but it's different every time. In the last one, they had to smuggle me into a church dressed like a baby in a carriage."

Andy started to laugh. "The ole baby in a monastery routine. It's a classic."

"I still like the 'they went that way!' fake out, where the guards think you went left, and you actually went right," said Hook Foot as he swung his hook off the bed.

Big Nose pointed to Andy. "Hey, yeah! We better teach that one to the newbies."

"Definitely." Andy snapped his fingers. "And we have to show them Mannequin Shenanigans! That's such a great one. You steal away into a shoppe and then hide out in some of the mannequin displays. Two plans ago, Vlad and I had to wear giant hats, but Vlad refused to take his helmet off first." All the guys in the tent laughed.

"What about Wa-Gone? Do you guys know that move?" Flynn asked, and the guys looked at him blankly. "The ole wagon switch-eroo? No?" He'd learned about this move in *Flynnigan Rider and the*

Secret of Calypso Cove. Apparently it wasn't popular with this crew.

He cleared his throat. "So what are these plans actually for? Like, what's the end goal?"

"Don't get ahead of yourself," Hook Hand said. "We will teach you all there is to know. As long as you do what you're told, everything will be fine." He bared his teeth at Flynn. "So, you know, don't mess up."

Flynn smelled his breath and took a step back. "Ever try chewing on mint leaves? Seriously, they do wonders."

"Hook Hand, give him a break." Andy stepped between them. "Flynn will be fine. He got the key, didn't he?" The other men shrugged or nodded. "I'm training him, and Atilla will be training Lance. They're going to do great."

"You mean we're not training together?" Flynn tried not to sound disappointed.

"The Baron said you and Lance have different specialties," Andy explained. "And he's got Atilla and Lance cooking up something important."

"Funny, Lance didn't mention anything," Flynn mused. They'd barely had time to talk at all since they'd been so busy with their other tasks. Lance had already earned a nickname—Culinary Genius. He'd gotten so good at directing the kitchen staff, all their meals were on time now.

"Culinary Genius is a busy guy," Big Nose said. "Speaking of which, anyone else headed over to the mess tent for breakfast? Or are you guys getting in on that morning game of cards Hook Foot is running before the first show?"

"No way," said Hook Hand as he rose his hook high in the air and almost got it caught on the wire the lanterns were hanging on. "Last week I lost my whole week's pay to Vedis."

Vedis. Flynn held his breath for a second. "This Vedis . . . You guys haven't introduced me to him yet, have you?"

"Nope! Other than the occasional card game, Vedis is pretty much a ghost," Big Nose said. "He keeps to himself." He scratched his sniffer. "Come to think of it, he's the only one who doesn't participate in the Baron's plans. Not sure why, but the Baron seems to have a soft spot for him. He really trusts the guy with animal training and stuff."

A ghost. That would explain why he hadn't seen the Man with the Mark since he arrived. He had to meet him. "Maybe I will play in this card game, fellas," Flynn said, rubbing his hands excitedly.

Big Nose snorted. "With what money? Better luck next week, Flynn."

"Can I come watch, then? Be an observer?" Flynn tried. "Learn the ropes?"

"Nah. The other guys don't like men looking over their shoulders," Big Nose said as he tied up his boots.

"I'll be as quiet as a mouse. As still as a . . . uh, dead tree in the woods." Okay, not the best analogy.

The other guys looked at him.

"Sorry. Not how we play," Big Nose said. "Why do you want to watch so badly anyway?"

Andy, Hook Hand, and Hook Foot looked at him. Flynn hesitated. "I wanted to meet Vedis. He, uh, looks familiar. I feel like he's maybe a friend of the family."

Andy looked confused. "Aren't you an orphan?"

"Yes, but all orphans come from someplace," Flynn said as they continued to stare at him. "He looks like someone my, uh, parents knew." Okay, his lie was getting worse. "I'd love to chat with him. Learn more about him."

"Vedis has been here as long as I have, which is a few years. . . ." Andy scratched his head.

"He's not really a talker either," Big Nose said. "Unless he wins King's Table. Or the elephant learns a particularly tough trick. Then he's in a really good mood."

"Animals. Hates small talk. Two things I know nothing about." Flynn sighed.

"I'll tell you what," Big Nose said, his gruff exterior seeming to thaw a little. "Come play King's Table next week after you make some money, and I'll try to seat you next to him."

Another whole week. Flynn tried not to be disappointed. "Thanks."

Andy put a hand on his shoulder and whispered in his ear.

"You're better off not playing. Everyone loses their shirt in a round of King's Table. Let's go eat and keep our shirts. I'm starving."

They weren't hungry for long. The kitchen crew had cooked enough eggs to feed the royal guard and then some. There was fresh bread and bacon and hot biscuits smothered with even hotter gravy. As Flynn followed Andy into the mess-hall tent to find a seat, he saw it was packed with people sitting at uneven tables and tree stumps for chairs. The sounds of forks scratching plates and laughter filled the air, as he took a metal cup and plate from a huge stack and followed Andy to a table where some of the others were already shoveling mounds of food into their mouths. It smelled divine.

"Flynn!" Lance called before Flynn could park his rear on a tree stump. He spotted his friend walking over with a frying pan full of hot bacon. Everyone jumped up, trying to get forkfuls, but Lance swatted them away. He was wearing a stained green apron that had seen better days, and his shirtsleeves were rolled up past his elbows. He looked hot and sweaty but equally happy as he dropped the frying pan on the table with a thud and sat down.

"Eat up! Fast! I practically had to risk my life to get you this," Lance said as Flynn speared several pieces of bacon and placed them on his plate. Seconds later, the others dove in, and soon the pan was empty. "Wait till you taste this bacon. I seasoned it with some spices before we started cooking. *Spices*, Flynn! No more slop for us."

"I could get used to eating like royalty," Flynn said as he quickly ate his bacon before the other men could steal it. "Wow, this is good. Really good! Lance, you're a genius. Is this maple I taste in here?"

"Yes, and a little brown sugar and chili powder," he said proudly. "Gives it a real kick."

"I'll say." Flynn looked at him. He felt like he hadn't seen his best friend since they were stuffed in that dragon cart. "No wonder you've been so busy."

"Sorry I haven't been around." Lance stabbed at some sausage on Flynn's plate. "Atilla has bumped me up to cooking at all three meals, and the kitchen staff has been showing me the ropes and different recipes. They've basically given me free rein to make what I want." He grinned. "Did you know they even gave me a nickname already?"

"Culinary Genius." Flynn buttered a biscuit and shoved a hunk in his mouth, hoping he didn't sound a tad envious. "I heard."

"Cool, right? I think the guys really like me — *us*," Lance corrected himself. "I'm really glad you suggested we join their crew. These guys really are a family, you know? And they've completely welcomed us into it."

Family. Flynn munched on a piece of bacon and thought again about Vedis and where a conversation with him might lead. He really had to tell Lance about him. "Listen, do you have a second? I have to tell you something important."

"Flynn!" Big Nose interrupted. He came rushing over with a plate piled high with biscuits covered in gravy. "King's Table game was called because we didn't have enough players, so Vedis is right over there." He motioned with his plate to a table across the room.

Flynn looked across the mess hall. A large man was eating quietly by himself at one end of a long table. His heart started to thump.

"You wanted to meet him, right? I can bring you over. He might talk to you if you hurry. He's going to eat fast and disappear again." Big Nose took a bite from his plate while holding it in midair.

"Who's Vedis?" Lance asked.

"Flynn thinks he might know his parents," Big Nose said, taking another bite of a biscuit without using his hands. Flynn paled.

"His parents?" Lance looked at Flynn, recognition dawning on him, and Flynn felt his stomach drop. "So that's why you wanted to come here," he whispered.

Flynn jumped up. "No, Lance. Let me explain."

"Lance!" Atilla yelled from across the mess hall. "You're needed, Culinary Genius!"

"I've got to get going," Lance said, turning away.

"Lance, wait." Flynn dragged him to the side of the tent, away from the others. "It's not what you think."

"Oh, really?" Lance sounded hurt. "Because what I think, *Flynn Rider*, is that you convinced me to leave Miss Clare's Home for Boys to join the circus because you saw someone who might know something about your parents. And that gave you an idea: If we join the circus and spend time around the guy, you might be able to finally track them down."

"Okay, so it's kind of like that," Flynn admitted. Lance turned to walk away, and Flynn grabbed his apron. "But I really do think this is the right place for us."

"*And* help you find your real family," Lance pointed out. Thankfully it was so loud in the mess hall that no one could hear them. "That's what this is really about!"

"No," Flynn said as Lance stared him down. "Although it is a bonus. Lance, this Vedis has the mark on his arm. The same mark that's on my letter!"

Lance's face softened for a moment. "Are you sure?"

"Positive. I saw it that day we were watching them work the moonstone cart in the village. He has a tattoo of it on his arm. He has to know what that mark means, and if he knows that, maybe he can tell me where the mark is from."

"Why didn't you just tell me?" Lance asked, getting upset again. "We're best friends. You could have told me the truth instead of hiding it from me. Not to mention telling Big Nose first."

Flynn hesitated. "I wanted to, but I didn't want you to think that this was the only reason I wanted to join the circus."

"Isn't it?"

"It's not," Flynn said. He heard a plate fall off a table and a group of men cheer. "I really think we could fit in here and see the world."

"Until you find your parents and leave me in the dust," Lance spurted out.

"You know I wouldn't do that," Flynn said, his heart beating faster. "You'd come with us."

"Yeah, because after they abandoned you, they're going to want to take you back plus one additional kid they don't want either," Lance snapped. Flynn took a step back in surprise, and Lance seemed to realize what he'd just said. "I didn't mean that . . . I . . ."

"Lance!" Atilla roared again.

"I've got to go," Lance said, not looking at Flynn again. "We're working on next week's menu, and then the guys are going to show me how to work a few of the other circus acts."

"Lance." Flynn's voice was pained. This wasn't good. Lance was mad. Really mad.

"Forget it," Lance said. "Good luck with Vedis." He wove through the tables and walked away.

Flynn knew better than to run after him. He needed to let Lance calm down, but he felt terrible. He wasn't sure he could even eat now, which was good because when he got back to the table his plate was empty.

Andy looked up at him. "What was that about?"

"Nothing." Flynn didn't want to talk about it. He looked at Big Nose. "So where is Vedis?"

"Sorry, Flynn," Big Nose said, sitting back and making a loud burp. "Vedis finished eating and left."

Flynn's heart sank. Great. He'd alienated his best friend and lost his chance with the Man with the Mark. And the day was only getting started.

TWELVE

"YOU WANT ME TO PUT ON A SHOW?
I'LL GIVE YOU A SHOW YOU WON'T FORGET."

—FLYNNIGAN RIDER IN *FLYNNIGAN RIDER AND THE HUNT FOR THE RED PEARL*

"Woo-hoo! It's payday! Everyone up!" Big Nose jumped out of bed, waking the others as a rooster crowed outside their tent.

Hook Hand yawned. "Let's make it a good one so the Baron is in an extra-good mood."

"He's announcing his new plan tomorrow; of course he'll be in a good mood," said Andy as he fluffed his pillow and turned over to go back to sleep.

Flynn looked over at Lance's empty cot and felt his stomach twist into knots. They hadn't spoken since their fight the day before. He knew he had some groveling to do, but when? Lance was busy with the kitchen staff and learning the ropes from his "crew," as he called it. Flynn's only hope was to pull Lance aside at the bonfire later (apparently they had one every payday). Their first paycheck would put them both in a good mood. Besides, they'd have to talk about the best way to get some money to Miss Clare.

For a moment he felt a wave of homesickness for Miss Clare's

Home for Boys. Were the others doing okay? Was Marius's adoption completed? Did anyone miss Eugene and Arnie?

"Flynn? You coming?" Andy pulled him from his thoughts. "We have to help Vlad get the chameleons out for some new number in the show."

"Where's Ulf? I thought he did that." Flynn stretched his arms wide, then grabbed his satchel and placed it over his shoulder. It was still empty, but he liked having it nearby. That, at least, felt right.

"Swim practice," Andy said with a shrug. "I guess the Baron wants to make sure we all know how to swim in case we ever have to cross a moat or something. Doesn't want anyone getting hurt."

That Baron was always thinking of his boys. Flynn really liked that about him.

But a short while later, Flynn was kicking himself for not suggesting breakfast before they transported the chameleon cages from the petting zoo area to the big tent. The cages were heavy and unwieldy. He wasn't sure he had it in him to carry the last two cages. Halfway to the big tent, someone barreled into his side.

"ROAR!" Sideburns shouted, knocking into Flynn and Andy and sending the cages tumbling.

"Hey!" Flynn cried as his cage landed sideways and the door burst open. The chameleon inside dashed into the bush before he could even react.

"Amélie!" Andy freaked, diving for the bush to search for the chameleon. Flynn got down on his hands and knees to look as well, as Sideburns and Patchy just laughed and walked away.

"Oh no, oh no, oh no!" Andy cried as he dug through the bushes. "Vlad is going to kill us if we don't find her! Amélie is his favorite!"

They searched for the next hour, but finally Flynn had to call it.

"I hate to say this, Andy," Flynn said gently, "but I have the feeling Amélie tasted freedom and isn't coming back." Andy moaned. "Come on, it's not that bad, is it? We have a dozen other chameleons. Vlad won't even notice."

"You don't get it. She was the smartest one of the bunch," Andy said woefully. "He taught her to climb carriages and buildings and even how to pluck stuff. He'll never find another chameleon like her."

"I'll go with you to tell Vlad what happened, if you want," Flynn said. He knew Vlad was intimidating even when he was in a good mood. "It is kind of my fault. Well, it's the Stabbies' fault, but maybe we can even find him a new frog to keep him happy. If you've seen one, you've seen them all, right?"

"Let's just get to the first show before it starts," Andy said glumly. "The Baron put us on dragon-cart duty together."

"Then let's make this the most ferocious dragon ever!" Flynn said. He was determined to make Andy smile. He even let him use the dragon bullhorn. Then they spent the next forty minutes throwing themselves against the carriage walls. Flynn even let Andy be the one to poke and prod the cage with paddles to make it sound like the dragon's tail was wagging. Andy got such a thrill out of it when they heard someone outside the carriage shriek.

For his part, Flynn was thankful he'd remembered to bring them both jugs of water. Between their paper fans and the cold drinks, he was almost comfortable in the hot wagon. The eager sounds of kids outside waiting for their turn to take a peek made things fun. And for a moment, he even forgot all about his problems with Lance.

"It's a real dragon!" a kid screeched and ran off.

Flynn swelled with pride and blared the bullhorn once more for good measure. He and Andy high-fived as the kids screamed again.

"That was a good show!" Andy pushed his sweaty brown hair out of his eyes and leaned against a stack of colorful uniforms that had arrived that morning. They looked strangely familiar somehow. "Thanks for taking my mind off Amélie."

"Amélie who?" Flynn joked. The show *was* a good one. Maybe he was getting pretty decent at this acting thing, even if he was only playing a dragon. He had a flair, didn't he? He knew that from his time with the boys at the orphanage, but realizing he could pull it off with strangers from inside a dark cart was pretty rewarding, too.

And yet . . . was being a showman enough of a skill for the Baron to keep him around long-term? Over the first week, he noticed different guys in his bunk had been given additional side tasks that no one talked about, but the Baron hadn't asked him to do anything. The night before, he caught Andy and Big Nose sneaking around with what looked like a map, and the day before that he heard Atilla talking about the blueprints of the castle. He wished he knew what all this stuff was for and why he wasn't being included yet.

His tentmates kept teaching him different moves they said he needed to know: the Heave Ho, the Drop and Stop, the Shoehorn Sam, the Bob and Weave, and the Lucky Eighteen, just to name a few. They were fun, but he still wasn't sure when he'd ever have a reason to use them.

Or whether he was even ready to try them. Flynn heard the other guys chat about their hauls from the shows each day during dinner. One night, everyone was talking about Ulf's big grab from the day before — an emerald ring that had slipped from a woman's finger after she tried to apply the slippery moonstone tonic and it fell off, unnoticed. He and Lance may not have been talking, but he could read his best friend like a book, and he knew, on the rare occasions Lance was there to hear the talk, he was as uncomfortable as Flynn was. Wasn't that just plain stealing? Didn't that make it wrong? Or was the Baron right — sometimes you just had to do what you had to in order to survive?

The Baron had actually come by the tent to check on both Flynn and Lance the day before. "You've both been doing some great work. We're so happy you're here," he'd said. No one had ever looked out for them like this before, other than Miss Clare. So why did Flynn still feel like something was missing from his life? Deep down, he knew it was Lance.

"And that's a wrap!" Andy said, pulling Flynn from his thoughts. The dragon line had finally dwindled, and they could hear the show in the main tent starting. "Better get out there and see what else we can pull off today," Andy said good-naturedly. "Want to team up?"

"I don't want to cramp your style," Flynn said, feeling anxious at the thought. "I'm just going to float around and see what strikes me. I'm sure I'll find something."

"Good luck out there," Andy said, slipping out of the wagon before him. "You know you've got to show up with at least one thing for the Baron this week."

Flynn froze. "I didn't know that."

What was he going to do?

Lance would know, he thought glumly. Whenever he had a problem he couldn't solve on his own, Lance was the one who helped him walk through the steps till they could come up with a solution together. But now they weren't talking.

"Hey, Andy?" Flynn called, and Andy turned around. "Maybe it would be better if we teamed up."

Andy grinned and practically skipped back over. "Excellent! Where should we start? Want to look for the swankiest folks in the ticket line or bump into someone so they drop their wallet?"

Flynn paled. "Uh . . . is there a third option?"

Andy gave him a look. "Look, Flynn, I like you, but we've all got to pull our weight! It's like the Baron says, these people don't even care enough about their stuff to realize it's gone. Meanwhile, we need it to keep the circus afloat. You can do this. You don't want to be bumped."

Exiled? Flynn certainly didn't want that. What would Lance say then? He'd forced his friend to leave the only home they'd ever known, and now Flynn was in danger of getting them canned? No. He couldn't have that. Besides, he couldn't leave this circus knowing Vedis might have a clue about his family. Flynn sighed and looked across the plains at the castle in the distance. Inside were a king and queen who would give anything to find their daughter. *Anything.* Was he so different from them? "You're right. Help me find my first mark."

"That's the spirit!" Andy said encouragingly. "Start small. Try sweet-talking. That's how I got a leather wallet yesterday. It was empty, but still. The fellow I was talking to was so distracted, he left it behind at the booth."

"So sweet-talking, huh? That's my in?" Flynn asked. Andy nodded. "Well, I guess I do have this one move I've been trying to perfect that might work."

"What is it?" Andy leaned on a barrel of fresh water for the animals.

"I call it The Smolder," Flynn said, "but it doesn't always work."

"Try it on me, and let me be the judge."

"On you?"

"Yes!" Andy insisted.

"Fine." Flynn rolled his neck a few times, then turned around quick and squinted at Andy while keeping his face down. Then he softly bit his lip. "Hi there. How you doing today?"

Andy burst out laughing.

"You try it if it looks so easy!" Flynn said, his face burning.

"Definitely do *not* do The Smolder!" Andy held his stomach and tried to quiet himself. "Just smile and flip your hair a bit. You've got good hair."

Flynn touched his head. "You think?"

"Definitely. Staylan seems to like it."

Flynn's face burned again. "What? Staylan? No. She won't even talk to me."

"I've seen her looking at you," Andy said. "Whatever you're doing works on her, so try it out on someone like . . . *her*." He pointed to a girl walking with her family.

Flynn turned. A girl around his age was pulling her mother through the crowd. She was dressed in a high-end petticoat gown adorned with lilac ribbons, and her mother was carrying a parasol. Two younger girls trailed them in matching dresses that looked way too heavy for the weather. All of the women had their hair done up in curls and ribbons.

Jackpot.

"Can we see the dragon?" the girl asked, her pleas bordering on whining. "Please? I want to go twice! Gretchen went yesterday and said there's definitely a real dragon in there. Can we? Please? Pul-eeze?"

Something flashed on the girl's wrist, blinding Flynn. It was a gold bracelet with jade jewels. Wasn't that similar to the bracelet the Baron once wanted to pluck and didn't? Flynn's heart beat faster. If there was ever an item to score for the Baron, this was the one.

"She's perfect," Andy whispered in his ear. "Go get her." He pushed Flynn into the crowd, and Flynn faltered.

"Tickets! Step right up!" he heard Staylan say.

That gave him an idea. He slipped into the ticket booth to beat the family to the window. "Hi there," Flynn said, and Staylan turned around. "Is your dad around?"

"He's busy working," Staylan said without looking at him. "Shouldn't *you* be? TICKETS!"

"That's why I'm here," Flynn said. The girl and her family were inching closer. He needed to be the one to wait on them. "Can you talk for a minute?"

"Kind of busy — TICKETS! Get your tickets!"

Flynn drew closer and whispered in her ear, "I need you to say you're sold out."

Staylan's violet eyes flashed. "Sold out? Why would I do that?"

"Just say it to the family approaching the window about the dragon cart — please?" Flynn hoped he looked endearing. "The daughter has something on her that I think your father will really like, but I need to motivate her to talk to me."

Staylan rolled her eyes. "That's for sure."

"So you'll do it?" Flynn begged. Staylan looked at him and said nothing. This called for drastic measures. He lowered his chin, looked up at her with puppy dog eyes, and bit his lip.

Staylan snorted. "What's wrong with your face?"

"Nothing," Flynn said, feeling foolish. "Just tell them you're sold out. I'll owe you!"

"Darn right. And I'll be collecting. I never forget a favor," Staylan said.

Flynn pulled several dragon-cart tickets off the stack without her noticing and slipped out of the booth again. Heart beating fast, he stood to the side as the girl and her family approached the window. He watched as Staylan backed up his story.

"I can't believe it's sold out! I see the line right over there!" the girl said to her mother.

"The main ring is starting shortly. Just forget the dragon cart and come watch," her mother pleaded, sounding tired already as the younger girls pulled on her arms.

"No." The girl folded her arms across her chest. "I'm waiting here to see if they sell anyone else dragon tickets." She eyed the booth again. "If they do, I'm demanding they sell me one, too." Her mother shook her head and walked away with the other girls.

Now was the time to make his move.

"Hi there." Flynn grinned wide as he ran a hand through his hair. "How are you doing?"

The girl side-eyed him. "Fine."

"I see you're waiting for dragon-cart tickets." Flynn's mouth was beginning to hurt from smiling so wide. "Too bad they're sold out for the day."

"The whole *day*?" The girl threw her head back. "That's the only reason I'm here! Why else would I want to watch a stupid circus?"

Stupid circus? Now he felt no guilt at all. He pulled the tickets out of his breeches pocket. "It just so happens that I have a few right here."

Her brown eyes widened. She reached a hand up to touch one, and Flynn pulled it away.

He started to relax. He was born to play the role of Flynn. He just had to bring the performance home. "Not so fast. Priceless tickets like these are going to cost you."

"How much do you want?" she asked, opening her change purse.

"I don't know." Flynn tapped the tickets against his chin. He could see Staylan watching him from the ticket booth. "These could go for a lot. Have you ever seen a live dragon? Nothing like it. Enormous. Kind of scary getting close to the wagon, but definitely worth it. See these scars?" He showed her a mark he'd gotten at breakfast earlier that week when Lance accidentally singed his arm with a frying pan.

(Back when they were still speaking.) "Got this feeding the dragon." He shuddered. "You do not want to have them breathe fire on you."

"Wow," she said, staring at his arm.

"These are in high demand," he said. "And I've got the last ones."

"Name your price," she told him.

Flynn pretended to think for a moment. He shook his head. "No, I think I'll just hold on to 'em. Thanks anyway." He started to walk away.

"Wait!" he heard her yell, and he couldn't help but grin.

He had her hook, line, and sinker.

"Please! I'll pay triple," she said, handing over all the coins in her purse. Silver flashed in the sunlight as she dropped them into her palm.

Suddenly, Flynn had a new idea. Maybe he didn't actually have to steal anything. He spotted Andy across the way talking to a family and made his decision. "I don't want your money. What about a trade? These tickets for . . . your bracelet."

The girl instinctively placed her hand over the jewelry. "My bracelet? Why would you want that?"

Flynn felt himself starting to sweat. "My mother had one just like it, but she had to pawn it for . . . to . . . uh, pay for me to travel to join the circus. I've always felt bad about that."

"Wow," the girl said, still holding on to the bracelet. "That's sad."

"It is," Flynn said. "Very sad. Tragic, even. She loved that bracelet! I wish I could replace it for her and be a good son."

The girl hesitated. She looked down at her wrist, then at the tickets in Flynn's hands again. "All right. You have a deal."

"Really?" Flynn gasped in surprise. "You'll trade?"

"Yeah, I found this old thing in my sister's drawer anyway." She snapped it off her wrist and handed it to him. "She won't even notice it's gone! And I get three tickets all for myself! Now hand them over."

Nice girl, he thought and forked over the tickets. She squealed with glee. "Just remember not to get too close to the peephole. Don't want to get scorched."

"I won't," she said, her eyes on the tickets as she ran off after her family. "Wait till I show them what I got! Mother!"

Flynn turned around, his heart beating fast as he searched for Andy. When he spotted him, he held up the bracelet, and Andy cheered.

He was now the proud owner of a jade bracelet.

For a few hours, at least.

THIRTEEN

"I PITY THE MAN WHO TRIES TO COME BETWEEN
A MAN AND HIS GOOD HAIR DAY."

—FLYNNIGAN RIDER IN *FLYNNIGAN RIDER AND THE BURIED TREASURE*

Payday really was a celebration.

Not only was a bonfire raging by nightfall and two pigs roasting on a spit, word was there were a dozen assorted pies for dessert, fresh sourdough bread with fig spread, and enough mashed potatoes to be molded into a mountain. A few men were engaged in a lively game of King's Table while Ulf played his lute. Others were singing and dancing while Atilla started passing out cupcakes before supper. If Flynn wasn't mistaken, even the Stabbington brothers appeared to be smiling.

It should have been the best night ever, but there was one problem: He and Lance still weren't speaking. Any time he'd get remotely close to his friend, Lance would make some excuse and walk away. Or he'd pretend not to see Flynn standing there. If Flynn had to hear Lance laugh heartily and say something like, "Atilla, stop! You are the funniest guy ever!" one more time, he was going to choke on a chicken bone.

"Happy payday, crew!" the Baron crowed as he made his appearance with Staylan at his side. He couldn't help but notice the sack in her arms.

Their weekly pay.

"I'm proud of each and every one of you," the Baron continued. "This has been a tremendous first week! Thanks to our parades far and wide through the kingdom, Staylan has calculated we've seen almost a quarter more visitors than we did in Aberdeen last month! And we still have five more days of shows ahead of us! I'm liking it here so much, we may just have to put down roots and stay!"

Flynn looked across the way at Lance. He was standing with the kitchen crew. The tall guy next to him whispered something to him, and Lance laughed. What was so funny? That's what Flynn wanted to know, but he couldn't catch Lance's eye.

The Baron stared at his crew. "Before we get to some housekeeping about the final shows in this kingdom, who has something grand to offer from today's shows to help our family thrive?"

Andy nudged him. Flynn felt his palms begin to sweat. He didn't want to go first. Instead, he watched as Ulf handed over another strand of pearls and Hook Foot bragged about hooking himself a beaded bracelet with hand-painted beads. Andy had found actual money—a sack of coins someone had dropped on their way out of the circus that afternoon, which elicited cheers from all.

"We've got one better!" Atilla spoke up, and Flynn watched as he and Lance stepped forward. Lance had a sack in his hands, which he emptied onto a table near the lavish spread.

"A set of gold flatware," Lance explained. "A family brought it with them for a picnic today and left it behind with their trash."

"Lance was the one who spotted it," Atilla said, sounding proud as he threw his arm around him. Lance smiled.

"That could be the catch of the day," the Baron said, touching the prongs on the bright gold fork.

"Go, team!" Atilla said as he and Lance high-fived.

Flynn felt his stomach turn, and he was pretty sure it wasn't from the sweet roll he scarfed down that afternoon.

"Patchy's got one better," Sideburns growled as he and his brother stepped forward. They placed a pair of dangly earrings styled like fleur-de-lis in the Baron's hands, and the men started to applaud.

"No one ever gets a whole pair!" Andy whispered to Flynn. "Wonder how they pulled that off."

The Baron held the earrings up to the light and grinned. "I take back what I said before — *these* are it!"

The Stabbies grinned at each other. Across the way, even Lance was cheering for the boys. Flynn couldn't stand it anymore.

"Actually, I have something for you, too!" Flynn stepped forward.

"His first score!" the Baron told the group, and people applauded. "I've been waiting to see what you'd come up with, Flynn." He smiled pleasantly. "Let's see what you've got."

"Something you've wanted for a while, I believe." Flynn opened his satchel and pulled out the bracelet. A quiet came over the group.

The Baron's face opened up in surprise. "Is that . . . ?"

"A jade bracelet. Yes." Flynn placed it in the Baron's hands. "I know you've been looking for one like it for a long time."

The Baron held the jade bracelet up to the light, and his eyes grew misty, though that could have been on account of the smoke. He looked at Flynn again. "How did you . . . Where did you . . . What in the name . . . I can't believe you remembered what I said."

He'd rendered the Baron speechless! *Take that, Stabbies! How do you like me now, Lance and Atilla?* "I listen to everything you say," Flynn told him. "When I saw it at the first show, I knew I had to get it, sir. I hope you like it."

"Like it?" the Baron's voice boomed in the night air. "This is the best score anyone has gotten since we arrived. No, since we've traveled the past three kingdoms!" He pulled Flynn close and hugged him. The crew cheered.

Flynn snuck a glance from under the Baron's arm. Staylan was watching, a slight smirk forming on her face. Andy grinned. Lance and Atilla had disappeared into the crowd. The Stabbingtons were glowering.

As the men continued to clap, the Baron looked at him. "Let's hear it for Flynn Rider!"

"Flynn Rider!" the crew crowed.

Flynn beamed. He had done it. He'd proven his worth. His status at the circus was secure. And he had to admit — the adulation was kind of appealing.

Plus, he was about to get paid for his work! The Baron sat down behind a table with Staylan next to him as he doled out coins. One by one, the men came up and collected their share.

"You really impressed the Baron," Andy whispered. "He's going to love you for life now! Well, at least till the next kingdom."

Flynn looked up in time to see Atilla and Lance collect their pay. Flynn attempted a smile.

"Hey, Andy," Lance said, ignoring Flynn.

Flynn frowned. How long was Lance going to freeze him out?

"Hey, Lance!" Andy waved and looked at Flynn again. "What's up with you two? It's like you're a ghost when he's around."

"We're fine," Flynn said as they moved up in the line, not wanting to get into it. "Just a small disagreement." Flynn stepped forward and faced the Baron.

"Flynn!" the man said happily as if he hadn't seen him in a while. He dropped the coins into Flynn's outstretched hand. "I just have to say it again — I'm really proud of you. Great job this week!"

"Thank you, sir," Flynn said, looking from the Baron down to his hand in awe.

There were half a dozen pieces of silver and one gold coin. He was rich! He'd never ever had a coin of his own before, and now he had several! Flynn shifted the coins back and forth in his palm for a moment, listening to them clinking together before he closed his fist and carefully placed the coins into a pocket in his satchel. He needed to find one of those little velvet sacks the other guys had to keep their money in. But now that he had his own, he and Lance could help out Miss Clare's Home for Boys!

Except . . .

If he and Lance weren't speaking, how were they supposed to combine their pay and get it to Miss Clare?

Behind him, Ulf had broken out into a dance while someone played the lute. Andy joined the others dancing.

"Come on, Flynn!" he called.

As happy as Flynn had been moments before, suddenly he found himself wanting to be alone.

"I'll catch you on the next song!" Flynn said slowly, backing away from the celebration, dipping into the shadows. He walked through the quiet camp till he reached the outskirts and the rocky terrain where he and Lance had hid that first night. It all felt so long ago now. Flynn took a seat on the nearest rock, placed his satchel next to him, and looked out at the darkening sky. Even though he could still hear the party, he felt completely alone. He'd really screwed things up with Lance.

Flynn felt a yank on his shoulder and turned around. The Stabbingtons had stolen his satchel!

"What do you have in here, Rider?" Sideburns asked, tossing the bag to Patchy, who opened the bag.

"Nothing at all! Want to pass that over, fellas?" Flynn tried to keep his nerves out of his voice, but it wasn't working.

Patchy put his hand in the satchel, pulled out the coins, and showed them to Sideburns.

"That's my first week's pay," Flynn said, "and I'm kind of fond of keeping it."

Sideburns shook his head. "Too bad. Patchy says you owe us one."

"Patchy said that?" Flynn couldn't take his eyes off his satchel. He had to get it back. Maybe if he could keep them talking, he could figure out how. "What else did Patchy say?"

Sideburns pursed his lips. "That you need a haircut and that you talk too much."

"I take insult to the hair part." Flynn reached in his pocket. "And I need that satchel back. I'll tell you what. We'll flip for it." He pulled out the two-headed coin the Baron had given him. "Double my pay — next week's included — or nothing. What do you say?" He went to toss the coin in the air.

Sideburns laughed. "That's so a Baron move. He gave you a two-headed coin, didn't he? Not going to work on us, Rider."

Flynn paled. Guess the coin wasn't so great after all.

The brothers stepped closer. "Where is your other half anyway?" Sideburns asked. "This is about him, too."

Flynn looked down. "He's not here."

"Aww, trouble in paradise? Not a surprise. Neither of you are trustworthy. And if we can't trust you . . . well, living and working together sure is going to be uncomfortable."

Flynn swallowed hard. "Fellas, listen, I think we got off on the wrong foot. If this is about the key, it wasn't personal."

Sideburns and Patchy looked at each other. "Patchy says it felt personal."

Flynn tried again. "Okay, so would you ask Patchy what I can do to make it up to you guys?"

"Give us yours and Lance's first week's pay," Sideburns said as Patchy counted the coins.

"Forget Lance!" Flynn snapped. He might have lost his money, but he wasn't losing Lance's, too. "Who needs him? I'm the one you want to deal with."

A fly buzzed around the brothers' heads, hissing loudly. Patchy finally reached up and snatched it in one fist, then dropped its carcass to the ground.

"I really want us to get along, fellas," Flynn tried. No, he *needed* them to get along so that he and Lance weren't constantly looking over their shoulders, waiting to be double-crossed. He needed to fix this. "Please? There must be something I can do other than pay you." Sideburns opened his mouth. "And I do mean *I*. You don't need Lance. I don't want him around and neither do you. Trust me." That would put them off, he hoped.

"Fine. Find another jade bracelet and give it to us," Sideburns said. "Patchy likes the color green."

"Who doesn't? Or priceless gems, but I haven't seen anything like that bracelet before, so the odds aren't great. Anything else I can do for you? Help Patchy learn how to speak?"

Sideburns revealed less than perfect teeth. "Patchy wants you two to take our swine duty."

Now it was Flynn's turn to be stumped. "Swine wha?"

"You really want to bury the hatchet?" Sideburns clarified. "Help feed the swines and clean up their pens before lights-out tonight."

Flynn frowned. "Sounds smelly, and I'm not a huge fan of being smelly."

Patchy grunted. Sideburns inched closer. "Patchy says, 'Do you want to make amends or not?'"

Flynn sighed. Feeding pigs and getting his hands dirty were two things that were not simpatico in his book. But did he really have a choice? If he wanted to keep Lance out of this, he had to do it. "Fine, but this counts for both Lance and me."

Sideburns sneered. "Deal."

Flynn slid off the rock and held out his hand. "Satchel, please. *And* the coins."

Patchy sighed and handed them over.

"Thank you. Now, where do I have to go?"

"Find Vedis," Sideburns said. "Tell him you're filling in for us, and — "

Flynn tried to not to smile. "Did you say Vedis? *The* Vedis?"

Sideburns just stared at him. "Yeah."

Flynn's heart started to beat quickly, and he got a funny taste in his mouth. This was his chance! "Say no more! I will clean those swines till they shine! Then we're even! Bye, fellas!"

Flynn broke out into a run. He'd just rounded the first wagon when he banged into something. *Someone,* rather. He looked up in surprise. "Lance."

FOURTEEN

Lance's face was stony. "So . . . now you're making deals with the Stabbington brothers on my behalf?"

"No," Flynn said quickly. "It's not what you think. I — "

"Save it!" Lance's left eye twitched. "I *heard* you, Flynn. 'We don't need Lance. I don't want him around and neither do you.'"

Lance had it all wrong. "No, Lance, I was just — "

Lance put up his hand. "And here I was coming over to talk to things out with you. I don't know why I bothered. Our friendship is over! Enjoy your new family, Flynn." He turned and started walking away.

Flynn went after him. "Wait!" He'd almost caught up to Lance when he got knocked to the ground. He looked up. It was the Stabbingtons getting in his way again. "Fellas, we have to stop meeting like this."

"Stop dawdling, Rider, and get over to Vedis before we get called out for being late," Sideburns growled.

He looked from Lance's retreating figure to the brothers again and sighed. There was no way they were going to let him go after Lance now. He didn't like it, but he'd just have to find Lance later at the bonfire and try to explain himself. The knocks against him were starting to pile up, but maybe he could still turn things around after he talked to Vedis. "I'm going. I'm going."

Flynn got up (with no help from the Stabbies, of course) and hurried through camp as the sounds of music and merriment at the bonfire made him feel ever lonelier. Finally, he reached the animal pens and Vedis's tent on the far side of camp. The tent flap was down, and he could hear people talking inside, so he hesitated before entering. One of those voices was the Baron's.

"Vedis, it will be just like the Spire Vault," he was saying. "Trust me. No heavy lifting."

"Like in the Forest of No Return?" Vedis asked. "Because we can't pack up the animals and have them sit in cages for days while you ride around in circles."

"We won't. This is a quick job. You can set off early that morning to the next kingdom, and we will meet you by nightfall. I promise, friend."

Flynn leaned closer to the tent flap to hear more, when the tarp flew open.

"Rider!" The Baron clapped him on the back. "What are you doing here? You should be off with the others, celebrating."

Should he tell the Baron how much he was enjoying the sudden use of his new name being shortened to Rider? Probably not. "I'm on cleaning and feeding swine duty, sir," he explained.

The Baron raised an eyebrow. "I thought that was Sideburns's and Patchy's job this week." Flynn stayed quiet. "Oh, right. I know you boys make deals on the side, so I'll stay out of it, but don't let them run the show, you hear? They give you any trouble, you come see me."

They were already giving him trouble, but something told him telling the Baron would only make the situation worse. "Thanks, sir."

"Flynn," he said with a laugh. "How many times do I have to tell you to just call me the Baron like everyone else. We're family!" He patted his back again. "Have fun helping Vedis." He leaned in close. "You might want to take a clothespin off the line and keep it on you. The stench in some of those pens is the worst." The Baron lifted the flap of the tent. "Vedis! You have help waiting!"

Flynn started to sweat. "I will, sir — I mean, Baron." He nipped a clothespin from the nearest tent line near a wagon and took a deep breath. This was it. The moment that could change everything. He was finally going to learn what that mark on Vedis's arm — and the one on his letter — actually meant. He patted his pocket to make sure the letter was still there. All that was left to do was ask.

He took a step forward and faltered.

What if Vedis claimed the tattoo was a birthmark?

Or said it was none of Flynn's business?

Even worse: What if Vedis knew nothing about the mark at all?

He wasn't sure he could handle that, but he had no choice. He had to keep going.

Flynn ducked inside and was immediately overwhelmed by the smell of dank hay and mud. Goats mulled about in pens, munching from troughs, as geese jumped in and out of a large metal pan filled with water. Several large pigs were fighting for room in front of a large empty trough. Vedis emerged out of the shadows, carrying a bucket.

"Who are you?" He had a deep yet soft voice and was wearing a sleeveless leather vest that showed off the mark on his arm perfectly. Flynn felt his heart beat faster. Up close, he knew for certain that the mark matched the one on his letter.

"Flynn Rider. I'm filling in for the, uh, Stabbington brothers." He couldn't take his eyes off the tattoo.

"Take the bucket. The pigs need feeding."

Flynn choked down a gag. The bucket was filled with old table scraps, and flies were buzzing around it. He stared at Vedis's retreating figure as he went back to the horses on the other side of the tent.

Talk to him, he told himself. If Lance had been there and still his friend, he'd have pushed Flynn over to the other side of the tent by now. Alone, Flynn wasn't sure what to do. Riding a horse made him nervous. Talking to the Weasel was intimidating. But asking Vedis a question that could change his whole life? That was downright terrifying.

"So you're Vedis, right?"

Vedis picked up a rake and began moving hay around the horses' stalls as if he hadn't heard him.

Flynn tried again. "Have you been here long? My friend Lance and I just got here last week. We're orphans. I guess a lot of the guys are. Do you have any family?"

Vedis continued raking.

Just keep talking, he told himself. *You're good at talking. Sometimes.* "I guess the circus is your family, right? That's kind of why we wanted to join after meeting Andy — do you know Andy? He's around my age — and he told us about the circus. Everyone needs a home. I've never had one. Well, I kind of did at the orphanage. My best friend really liked it there, but I wanted to find my family, and that led me here."

Vedis looked up for the briefest of seconds and then looked away again. He was intrigued. Flynn could tell. Flynn swatted a fly away and made his way closer to the horses. "I used to live at Miss Clare's Home for Boys. So did Lance. But we got too old, and it was time to move on." He pushed his hair out of his eyes and forced himself to keep going. "That's okay. We have big plans. Together. At least we did until . . . Lance is like my family, but I know I have another family out there somewhere, and I'm hoping to find them, too."

Vedis stopped raking and looked up again. "Do you always talk this much?"

Flynn couldn't stop now. "The thing is, when I was left at the orphanage as a baby, my family left a note saying to look after me." He raised his hand shakily and poked Vedis in the arm. "And on the bottom of the letter was the same mark as you have on your shoulder."

Vedis physically stiffened. "You should go feed the pigs."

"Please," Flynn said, holding on to a railing. "I just want to know what that mark means. Is it a place? A guard? A secret society? Or was someone just trying to draw a cat and forgot eyes? I need to know."

Vedis put down the rake and looked at Flynn, his blue eyes somber. "You don't want to know what this mark means. Trust me. No good can come of it."

"Not true! It would help me figure out where I'm from. It would give me a starting point." Vedis walked out of the pen, and Flynn followed. The geese and goats seemed to be watching them. "Why put the mark on the letter if it wasn't important?"

Vedis grabbed a jug of water and poured it into the bath the geese were splashing in. "We are not having this conversation."

"It's got to be important if you inked it on yourself." Flynn reached into his pocket and pulled out the letter. "Look! This is it right here." He pushed it under Vedis's nose. "This says something about my parents needing to send me away. Does the mark have something to do with the kingdom I'm from? Was my kingdom at war? Do you know an 'M' by any chance?"

Vedis's eyes scanned the letter quickly, and Flynn noticed Vedis flinch. "Forget it, kid. That mark is a symbol for something that no longer exists."

Flynn heard his heart beating in his chest. He was getting somewhere! "So the mark *does* mean something? Is it a country? A shoppe? Or are you in some sort of secret club that my family also belongs to?" Vedis glared at him. "Please. I just want to find my parents."

Vedis pointed to the mark. "If your parents have anything to do with this mark, they're . . ." His lip trembled. "Gone. I'm sorry."

Flynn felt his heart stop. "Gone?" he whispered. *As in dead?* Suddenly he didn't feel well. "You don't know that." Vedis was quiet. "How can you know that? How can you be sure?"

He grabbed Flynn's letter and pointed to the mark. "This right here is the mark of the Dark Kingdom, and that kingdom is no more." He pushed the letter back at Flynn's chest.

Flynn quickly folded it up and placed it safely in his pocket again. His hands were shaking. "But how could a kingdom just be gone? Kingdoms don't just disappear . . . do they?"

Vedis sat down on a wood log as if his legs were giving out. "The kingdom I came from was destroyed. Most people barely escaped the destruction caused by the Moonstone."

"Moonstone," Flynn repeated. "You mean like the tonic that we sell here at the circus?"

Vedis nodded. "I told the Baron stories about it, and he liked the name. Thought it sounded mysterious and magical. It's not. The real Moonstone swallowed the Dark Kingdom whole."

"Swallowed?" Flynn tried to picture a kingdom visibly being swallowed. He couldn't. "But you escaped. Others had to have as well, right?"

Vedis looked solemnly at Flynn. "Those who survived scattered. I don't think anyone stayed behind."

"Don't *think*, but they could have," Flynn said, clinging to hope. "So maybe someone is still there."

"Life can't be sustained there." Vedis shook his head. "All that is left is the Brotherhood." He pointed to the mark on his arm, "And I no longer belong to that either."

Flynn leaned forward. "Why? Why did you leave the Brotherhood? What is it?"

"Look, the stone destroyed everything our kingdom had—our homes, our royalty, and it cost us our future. I'm sorry." Vedis stood up. "If you're looking for someone from the Dark Kingdom, you're not going to find them." He handed him a pail with grain. "Here. For the goats."

Flynn looked at the bucket. "But . . ." That's it? There had to be more Vedis wasn't saying. He trailed after him, feeling desperate. "Would I find it on a map? Is it far from here? Do you know how to get there?"

Vedis looked at him sadly. "I'm sorry, kid. The Dark Kingdom can't be found."

FIFTEEN

"SECRETS? WHAT SECRETS COULD A GUY LIKE ME
POSSIBLY BE KEEPING?"

—FLYNNIGAN RIDER IN *THE TALES OF FLYNNIGAN RIDER*

The next morning, even the sight of sweet rolls at breakfast couldn't cheer Flynn up.

He finally knew what the mark was, and it was for a kingdom that didn't exist.

Did that mean his parents were gone, too?

Vedis had said some had escaped, which meant those people could be anywhere. They could even be visiting the circus that very day! If they did, would they all have marks like Vedis? He'd said something about them being part of the Brotherhood. What *was* the Brotherhood? Were his parents a part of it, too? Did Vedis possibly know his parents? How would Flynn even ask, not knowing a thing about them other than the fact they had given him up?

Which made him wonder again: *Why* did they send him to an orphanage? Could it have been they made it out and had fallen on hard times? If that were the case, then he'd help them get back on their feet. He just had to find them first.

"Hey, Flynn, are you going to eat that roll?" Hook Foot asked from across the table. "'Cause if not, I'll take it."

"Hey! I was going to ask for it!" Hook Hand grumbled.

"Well, you didn't ask fast enough," Hook Foot snapped.

The two started to argue, and Andy swooped in and stole Flynn's plate. The brothers quieted.

Andy smirked. "To be honest, you look a bit green, so I'd suggest you skip the roll this morning."

Flynn waved the roll away. "They can have it."

Andy put the plate down with a clang, and both Hook brothers reached for it. Hook Hand grabbed it with his hook, and the table erupted in applause.

Flynn wasn't sure he'd ever be hungry again. Hope of finding his parents was dwindling, and he'd royally screwed things up with the only family he'd ever known. Speaking of Lance, where was he? Atilla was going table to table with some sausage links, but he didn't see Lance anywhere. Flynn wanted to make things right with his best friend again. Why had he thought the circus was their way out into the world? It only dawned on him now that he didn't need the circus to find freedom. All he needed was Lance. Apologizing couldn't wait. He stood up fast, his knees knocking into the table and making everyone's water glasses rock.

"Sit down," Staylan said, placing a hand on his shoulder and using it to step onto the bench Flynn was sitting on. "Gentlemen! My father has an announcement to make! He'd like to see you all in the big tent before the first show." She glared at the men still seated with their breakfasts in front of them. "Now." She jumped down and walked out of the tent.

The men looked around and started whispering.

"Do you think something happened?" Vlad asked. "We still have several shows to do here."

"Maybe it's the guards," he heard Atilla say. "Could they be onto us? Do we need to move up the plan?"

Big Nose laughed nervously. "What if we're not ready? What if we can't do what he wants this time?"

"We have to," Andy said, sounding tense. "You know what happens if we don't."

Hook Hand shut his eyes tight. "I don't want to get on the Baron's bad side again."

Hook Foot started to shake. "Neither do I!" He started grabbing scraps from everyone's plates and shoving them in his mouth.

"Bad side?" Flynn was confused. "The Baron seems like a nice guy . . . other than when he's giving initiations, of course."

Big Nose snorted. "Flynn, you don't know him the way we do. He — "

"BIG NOSE!" Staylan shouted back into the tent. "Let's go!"

Everyone quickly filed out of the tent. Staylan stopped Andy and Flynn at the door.

"You two have a special assignment to complete in the next few days," she told them.

"Special assignment, huh?" Flynn instantly puffed out his nonexistent chest muscles, hoping it made him look bigger. He grinned at Andy as if to say, *You see? If the Baron was such a bad guy, he wouldn't give us an important assignment.* "What does the Baron need? Someone to distract the guests? No one can handle The Smolder."

Staylan stared at him blankly before reaching into a bucket at her feet and producing two brushes. "You two are on paint duty. Make the Baron's carriage look like this." She handed him a scroll. It had a drawing of an official carriage from the kingdom on it and color choices scribbled on the paper. It was the carriage the Baron rode on in the parade. That was odd. Why did he need a carriage that looked like one of the kingdom's? Flynn picked up a paintbrush.

"Not now, Flynn," Staylan said, rolling her eyes. "After my father speaks." She grabbed him by the front of his shirt and pulled him toward the tent. Andy followed.

They appeared to be the last two inside. Lance was already sitting with the kitchen crew. They made eye contact, then both looked away, then back again. But when Flynn tried to catch his eye again, Lance focused on talking to Atilla. Disappointed, Flynn sat with his roommates and waited for the Baron to appear. He did moments later, carrying a scroll.

"Crew! We've got our official invitation to perform at the Festival of the Lost Princess!"

The group applauded, and Flynn breathed a sigh of relief. They were going to perform for the king and queen? That didn't sound so bad. Is this what everyone was so nervous about?

"We'll need to cancel our last day of shows, but it will be well worth it." His grin widened. "As many of you will recall, it is almost six months to the day that Big Nose mentioned the Festival of the Lost Princess: the kingdom's day of festivities honoring the royal babe who was stolen from the king and queen while they slept." His eyes went to Staylan. "Immediately, I thought to myself: What kind of thief would steal someone's daughter? Whoever took this child should pay!"

Flynn clapped along with the others. Who knew the Baron had such a big heart?

"This year is the five-year anniversary of the princess's kidnapping. In all that time, there has been no clue as to her whereabouts. No leads. The king has sent out group after group to search for her, and they've turned up nothing."

Flynn felt a flutter in his chest. This princess, wherever she was,

was a lucky girl. What he wouldn't give for his parents to be doing the same thing. If they were alive, they would know exactly where Flynn lived . . . unless . . . Vedis's words echoed in his head. The whole kingdom was destroyed. Flynn inhaled sharply. He didn't want to think about the fact that they might *not* be around.

"The king and queen are afraid the people will eventually stop looking for their princess," the Baron continued, "which is why they are pulling out all the stops to make this the biggest festival yet! They are doing everything they can to keep their daughter in people's memories — and their hope alive — by offering a hefty reward for her safe return." The whites of his eyes seemed to get larger with each word. "And this isn't just any reward — it's every lavish gift the poor little lost princess has received from visiting royals, kingdoms, and dignitaries. We're talking gold, precious stones, pearls, shimmering bowls carved out of crystal, figurines, and goblets. There's even a gilded ostrich egg, so Ulf heard!"

"I didn't even know Ulf could talk," Andy whispered.

"Maybe he mimed it," Flynn cracked.

Flynn looked around. The crew's eyes were as big as saucers. They were licking their lips as if they'd been offered the world's largest steak in the finest establishment the kingdom had to offer. It was kind of funny. What were they getting so excited about? It's not like they'd already found the lost princess and were claiming the reward. Lance and Atilla were whispering with some of the others sitting around them. He willed Lance to glance his way again, but he didn't look up.

"So what do you want us to do? Find the lost princess?" Atilla piped up, seemingly hearing Flynn's thoughts.

The Baron sighed deeply as Staylan shook her head. "Atilla, aren't you listening? The child can't be found! Especially not after all this time."

"But you said all this stuff is being given as a reward!" Vlad clutched a unicorn figure in his left hand. "What good is a reward if we can't find the kid?"

The Baron's smiled greedily. "Who needs to find the child to claim the reward?"

Silence fell over the group.

"Crew, tomorrow, as the kingdom celebrates, we are going to take the reward for the lost princess right under their watch!"

Flynn felt his stomach drop. He looked around to see the others' reactions. None of them appeared as shocked as he was. This didn't make sense. The Baron said he took things that others left behind to help take care of them. In a way he was like Lance's idol, Lance Archer. Flynn could make his peace with that — taking from the rich, giving to those who needed it. But this was different. This was stealing reward money from a lost princess. Flynn instinctively looked around the tent for Lance. When his eyes found him, he couldn't figure out his friend's expression.

"But, boss, how are we going to do that when there are guards everywhere?" Big Nose squeaked.

"Don't worry about the details," he said casually. "All of you will be told the part you will play when you meet with me this evening. But know if we pull this off, not only will it be our biggest heist ever, I will be paying each of you ten times your usual weekly pay for a job well done."

Everyone started talking at once, the energy in the room igniting as each person thought of what they could do with the money.

"Ten times our usual pay?" Andy repeated, looking like he might fall off the tree stump he was sitting on in shock. "That's over two months' pay in one night!"

"That might be enough to buy a boat *and* help the orphanage all at once," Flynn said wistfully. If he and Lance combined all their earnings, they could get everything they'd ever wanted after one night.

One job. That's all that stood between him and a chance to save the orphanage and sail off to find his parents and this Dark Kingdom — or what was left of it — immediately.

How could he turn that down?

And yet, how could he not?

This was all wrong. The reward was meant to be a call to action, to help people find the lost princess. And the Baron was planning on stealing it for himself. What if their heist prevented someone from actually finding her and reuniting her with her family? He thought of the drawing he'd seen of the wide-eyed baby girl with the flowing hair. Flynn thought again of the king and queen, who he had only seen in portraits, standing forlornly on the castle balcony, wondering where their child was. Had his own parents ever done the same?

"I'll be calling you over individually throughout the course of the evening to let you know what part you'll be playing in tomorrow's events," the Baron said. "Go finish your breakfast, and I'll see you soon!"

Flynn filed out of the circus tent with Staylan and the other men, his thoughts tumbling through his head. He was so confused. Lance was just ahead of him. He rushed to catch up. He needed to talk to him, now more than ever.

"Flynn? Lance?"

Flynn turned around. The Baron was staring at them, his mustache curving downward in a frown. "I need to talk to you two."

Flynn glanced at Lance, but Lance's face was still blank.

"Sir?" Flynn asked. "Is something wrong?"

The Baron crossed his arms and stared hard at Flynn. "You tell me."

SIXTEEN

"I LOVE A GOOD BROTHERHOOD, SISTERHOOD, EVERYONE-HOOD.
JUST NOT A HOOD-HOOD, AS THEY MESS UP MY HAIR."

—FLYNNIGAN RIDER IN *FLYNNIGAN RIDER AND THE SECRET OF CALYPSO COVE*

Flynn took a step back. "Come again?"

"You found the key!" the Baron's voice took on a jovial tone, and Flynn felt his jaw unclench. "If you two hadn't gotten that key from the Weasel, this heist would not be possible. So thank you! It's because of you two that we're going to be richer than we ever imagined."

And there was that stomachache again. He hadn't realized the key was *the key* to the whole operation! "Sir?"

"Rider, enough with the sir! That key opens the door to the Antiquities Shoppe. Do you two know why that's important?"

"No, sir," Lance said, speaking for the first time.

"Because that's where the reward will be kept during the festival! And we now have the key that leads right to it."

Flynn paled. That meant if the Baron stole the reward, it would be all his fault. "Uh . . . you're welcome, I guess?"

The Baron burst out laughing. "Such a cutup, Flynn! This is why I wanted to talk to you two first. I have full faith in you boys, which is why I've decided to give you the plum role in this heist." His eyes glittered.

Flynn felt his heart start to palpitate. "Us? No! You're too generous. You don't have to do that!" He laughed nervously. "I'm already on paint duty, and besides, I'm sure you've got way more qualified guys working this job than us. Right, Lance?"

"What do you want us to do?" Lance asked, not looking at him.

"That's the spirit!" the Baron said, leaning in. "Here's how it's going to work: During the circus performance in the village, you and Lance, along with the Stabbington brothers, will knock out the royal guards on duty at the Antiquities Shoppe, where the reward will be on display, and take their place." He looked at Flynn. "The brothers will stay on lookout outside while you two slip into the shoppe and load up from the reward table. If our calculations are correct, you'll roll back out of the kingdom just as our performance is ending and find us at the meeting point before the next guard shift even starts. With the lighting of the lost-princess lanterns, everyone will be preoccupied, and we'll be long gone before anyone even realizes what's happened." He grinned. "It's the perfect plan!"

Flynn side-eyed Lance, then cleared his throat. "Wow, that's, uh . . . you've given us a big part in this. Kind of the only part."

"Well, there are many working pieces, but yes, you two are key," the Baron explained.

Flynn was sweating profusely now. "I hate to take away a job from someone else really worthy."

"Everyone takes the big risks at some point, Flynn, but no need to be nervous. I have faith in my newest men. I know you two won't let me down. We'll get into more details tonight at the bonfire, but I want to make sure you two understand what you need to do. Do you?"

Flynn wasn't sure what to say. Did he really have a choice? If he retraced his steps over the last two weeks, the signs were as clear as day: This was all his fault. If he hadn't wanted to find his parents so badly, he never would have suggested he and Lance join the circus to meet the Man with the Mark. If he hadn't convinced Lance to be part of the Baron's crew and make money, they wouldn't have agreed to steal the key. Now that they had done that, the Baron thought he could count on them for whatever horrible thing he was planning next — which was stealing from the king and queen.

The Baron sat back and looked at them. "Well?"

Going on a mission to get the key for the Baron was one thing, but stealing gifts meant to be a reward for finding the missing princess felt like wading into deeper, darker waters. He had to say something. The Baron was a sensible man — and a father! Maybe he could make him see reason.

"Sir, I don't know," Flynn said quietly. "Your plan is brilliant. Don't get me wrong." The Baron smiled. "But stealing treasure from a missing little girl feels wrong. Don't you think? You've got a kid yourself. If she were missing, wouldn't you want someone looking for her?" The Baron's expression changed. "There's got to be another way to make some extra money for the circus, like . . . like . . ." He looked desperately at Lance, who still wouldn't make eye contact. "Well, I'm not sure yet, but I'll come up with something."

The Baron's face darkened. "Flynn, I gave you a home here because I thought you understood the way things work. I introduced you to my family, who I take pride in taking care of."

"I know, I — " He saw the Baron's face change and knew he was in hot water. As he was quickly learning in this job, a man with no plan was a problem.

The Baron stood up, his voice rising. "I trusted you with this business and brought you and Lance into the fold. You know all our secrets now. You know the way things work and what we have going on here." He motioned to the tent around him. "Do you think a thriving business like this just happens?"

Flynn started to back away, horrified at the way this situation was turning on him. "No, sir, I just was thinking that this is a princess and she's missing and . . ."

"And what? Her life is more important than ours?" the Baron boomed. "Are you saying you're trying to walk away?" His face was now inches from his. "Because no one walks away from me. Not without paying a price." He was breathing so heavily Flynn could smell the mint he'd chewed on earlier.

So this was why everyone seemed so scared of the Baron at breakfast. His plans weren't simple snatch-and-grab jobs that no one was the wiser about. They were risky, I-might-wind-up-getting-hanged-for-my-crimes endeavors. No wonder the Baron wanted others to do his dirty work.

"We won't let you down, sir," Lance interrupted. "Don't worry. We know what has to be done."

The Baron backed away, his eyes still on Flynn, who was gaping at Lance.

Did Lance really see no problem with this?

"That's what I thought." The Baron sat back down and smoothed his long hair. "I expect the job done perfectly tomorrow, boys. Because if it's not . . ." He looked at each of them. "You will be answering to me."

"Yes, sir," he and Lance said together. Lance quickly exited the tent, forcing Flynn to struggle to catch him.

"You don't really want to do this, do you?" Flynn whispered.

"Not talking to you." Lance kept his eyes forward.

"Then don't talk." Flynn kept in time with him. "I'll do all the talking. I like talking! Lance, I know you're mad at me. I know I messed up, but you can't really be okay with this."

Lance squirmed.

"How can we steal reward money meant to help find the lost princess? This isn't like Lance Archer giving to the poor," Flynn pointed out. "This is stealing something huge just for the sake of getting rich. It's really wrong."

"Right or wrong doesn't matter. We work for the Baron now, thanks to you." Lance scratched his left eyebrow. "We need to do this."

Flynn pointed at him. "Ha! I saw you do it."

"Do what?" Lance scratched his eyebrow some more.

"Scratch your left eyebrow. You only do that when you're nervous! You don't want to do this either!"

"I don't scratch my left eyebrow!" Lance turned to look at him. "And even if I did, it doesn't matter. We have a job to do! So I'm going to get ready for the bonfire with the others — you know, the people who actually care about me and won't leave me behind. A real family is the one you make for yourself along the way, and I know where mine is now."

Flynn felt his heart stop. "You don't mean that. *I'm* your family. You know that."

But Lance just looked at him and started to walk away.

Lance had made his choice.

And so had he. He was alone now, but that didn't matter. Flynn wasn't sure how he was going to stop the Baron or the rest of the crew, but he would figure out a way.

SEVENTEEN

"LET'S FACE IT: THE ROAD AHEAD IS GOING TO GET ROUGH SOMETIMES. BUT IF YOU KEEP YOUR HEAD, STAY COOL, AND FLASH THEM A KILLER SMILE, YOU'LL BE OKAY."

—FLYNNIGAN RIDER IN *FLYNNIGAN RIDER AND THE LOST TREASURE OF SCOTIA*

L EAVING TOWN A DAY EARLY! SEE YOU NEXT TIME!
— The Great Baron and His Unusual Oddities

The hand-painted sign — still dripping wet — had been tacked to a tree near where the circus should have stood. The tents had already been taken down, the wagons were packed, the bonfire had been dismantled even though embers from last night's fire were still smoking, and any sign that the circus had been in the kingdom had been wiped away with the wind. They'd worked all night to get ready. Everyone was excited for the next stop. It was some place called Vardaros, which was known as the "City of Fun and Games." The Great Baron and His Unusual Oddities were leaving the kingdom behind. All that was left to do was perform one last time.

For Flynn, this would be the biggest performance of his life. He had to stop the Baron. He just wished he knew how.

"Everyone knows what they're supposed to do, right?" asked

Staylan as she climbed aboard her dad's wagon. "Then good luck, everyone! See you in Vardaros!"

Flynn felt a strong hand on his shoulder. He looked up. It was the Baron.

"Feeling better, Rider?" he asked quietly. The Baron was dressed in his ringmaster uniform, his hair slicked back neatly in a ponytail he only wore for performances.

Flynn tried not to let his legs shake. "Right as rain, sir."

The Baron's cool blue eyes seemed to see through him. "So no . . . doubts, correct? I'd hate to think you weren't fully committed here."

He knows, Flynn thought anxiously. He put on a brave face. "Fully committed, sir. No worries."

The Baron smiled coolly. "Then see you in Vardaros. Good luck today."

He climbed aboard his wagon after Staylan, and their wagon slowly pulled away, leaving tracks in the mud.

Andy gave a wave to Flynn from the wagon in front of him. "See you in Vardaros!" he said as he and Ulf rolled away.

"See you!" Flynn said, his stomach sinking as he waved good-bye. Andy had been good to him, and chances were they wouldn't cross paths again after today.

"Rider! Patchy wants to know if you're coming or not." Sideburns looked down at Flynn from the driver's seat.

Flynn hadn't realized it, but he was still standing alongside the wagon he was supposed to ride in, clutching one of the gold-painted wagon wheels. He looked up at him and Patchy. Lance was behind them, tying down the last part of the tarp, which concealed the wagon that had been painted to look like an official carriage of the kingdom.

"Well, when you put it so nicely, how could I refuse?" Flynn climbed aboard, side-eyeing Lance as he sat down in the only available seat next to him. Lance wouldn't look at him.

Before this, they'd never fought. Sure, they used to play pranks on each other at Miss Clare's Home for Boys. Lance was famous for stealing Flynn's comb and placing it somewhere impossible for him to find (like next to the garbage bin). And anytime Flynn saw a spider, it mysteriously wound up on Lance's pillow. But no matter who did the pranking, the end result was always the same: Both boys would yell for a moment, then marvel at the other's ingenuity. Their fights, if you could even call them fights, never lasted more than ten minutes.

But he wasn't sure they'd ever get over this one. This disagreement was huge. The only thing he couldn't understand was why Lance hadn't ratted him out to the Baron yet. To make matters worse, at some point that day, they'd have to square off. Flynn didn't like thinking about it. He just wished there was a way to make Lance see reason — he couldn't let the Baron steal the reward money.

Flynn sighed. Leaving the circus also meant he wouldn't have the money to help Miss Clare with the orphanage. *I'm sorry, Miss Clare,* Flynn thought as the carriage began to roll away. *Someday I'll find a way to make money to help you. You know, if I don't botch what's going to happen today and wind up in the castle dungeon for all eternity.*

But before he could come up with a single scenario that didn't end with him in cuffs or hung by his jacket in the middle of the desert to get his eyes pecked out by vultures, the main city rose to greet them.

From the roof of Miss Clare's Home for Boys, the castle was nothing more than a tiny dot on the landscape. Now that he was up close, Flynn could see how magnificent it truly was. Even Lance looked in awe as they headed toward the bridge that connected the kingdom to the mainland. The island was mountainous, with the castle sitting high on a hill surrounded by village homes and shoppes nestled among lush greenery and winding cobblestone streets. But the castle was clearly the centerpiece, its teal palace turrets reaching so high into the sky they looked taller than the puffy clouds marking the otherwise perfect afternoon weather.

"Wow, this place has a lot of security," Lance said, speaking for the first time since they'd shoved off. Flynn watched as Lance scratched his left eyebrow. "Look at all those guards."

Several guards were standing on the castle wall above them while more were lining up ships out on the water. How the Baron thought they could pull off a heist under the guards' watch was anyone's guess. *Could he want us to fail?* Flynn wondered. No. He wanted the reward, but he wasn't willing to take the fall for it either. The sudden clip-clop of horses made him look up.

More than a dozen guards atop white steeds trotted in formation toward their wagons. Every guard stared straight ahead, as did their horses, who were decked out in purple and gold sashes laid over their saddles. A sunburst medallion hung from their reins. Suddenly a pony broke from the pack and came cantering up to their wagon.

"Maximus! Maximus! Slow down!" he heard a guard shouting.

Flynn tensed as the pony stopped short, sniffing the air around the carriage. The horse looked around and made eye contact — which was eerie — then let out a loud neigh and rose back on his hind legs. Flynn's heart began thumping harder.

The guard caught up to the pony on his own horse and grabbed Maximus's reins with his free hand. "Maximus, they're part of the circus! Sorry!" he told the Stabbingtons. "We still need this pony to stop thinking every unknown wagon that goes by contains criminals."

The boys laughed nervously.

Maximus looked at Flynn knowingly and neighed again as the guard pulled him away. It was almost as if that horse could smell the deception on them. Flynn hoped he never crossed paths with him again!

With the coast clear, the Stabbies rolled over the bridge and into the village. Flynn forced himself to ignore the WANTED posters he saw along the way. (Many were for Lance Archer, but he could swear one was for someone who looked like Vlad.) Instead, he focused on the streets ahead. They were packed with people wearing their finest hats and dress wear as they perused shoppes under gold and purple banners decorated with sunbursts. Parents walked with children high atop their shoulders and pointed out all the decorations. People played music in the square while the wagons rumbled on, winding up the road filled with carts. They sold everything from flowers and treats to the lanterns that folks would launch into the sky in honor of the lost princess at the end of the festivities. Up until now, Flynn had only ever witnessed the lanterns from a distance.

"The circus is setting up over there, but we keep going." Sideburns pointed to the end of the square, where Flynn could see the Antiquities Shoppe. Then a flash of color drew his eye.

It was a large mural of the king and queen holding their infant daughter. The princess looked different than she did on the MISSING posters, where she was just a black-and-white outline. Here, she was in full color and looking like a real person. Her hair was the color of gold and her big, round eyes as green as the jade in the bracelet he had stolen for the Baron. Beneath the mural, people had placed flowers. Next to the display was a scroll on an easel stamped with the royal seal.

REWARD FOR THE SAFE RETURN OF THE LOST PRINCESS!

The king and queen would like to remind every citizen in the kingdom that the safe return of the princess will be greatly rewarded! Whoever finds their daughter will receive every gift the lost princess has ever received, for their greatest gift would be her safe return. The reward is on display at the Antiquities Shoppe this afternoon from 12 to 5 PM. The king and queen thank the people for their continued good wishes and hope for the princess's safe return.

Flynn wondered how the king and queen survived year after year, always hoping for the return of the person they loved most in this world. Were his parents out there, too, having survived the Dark Kingdom and had started over in the hopes of reuniting with their son?

Flynn's eyes bored into his best friend's head, almost willing him to wonder the same thing. More than anything, he wanted Lance to turn around and say, "You were right. Let's stop the Baron." Instead, Lance tapped Sideburns on the shoulder.

"Won't it look suspicious if we keep on while all our other wagons stop?" Lance asked.

"No," Sideburns hissed. "Just watch."

"Make way for the Great Baron and His Unusual Oddities!" shouted Andy, jumping from the cart up ahead and dressed as a court jester. "Don't miss the Great Baron, performing in the village square at sunset at the request of the fair king and queen! Honor the lost princess and see the final show before this traveling circus moves on to the next kingdom!" The bells on his hat jingled with each step he took. He turned around, saw Flynn, and winked as Flynn's wagon pulled ahead and rumbled farther down the street.

Andy's greeting was the sign they'd all been told to watch for.

The heist had officially begun.

"Listen closely, as every step you're about to hear has been carefully planned and timed," the Baron had explained the night before at the bonfire. *"Step one: Andy will jump off the first wagon and announce our arrival, touting every amazing feat of strength and awe that the people will see at our performance that afternoon."*

Flynn watched as Andy rattled off a long list.

"Your eyes will be amazed at the tricks performed by our exotic animals, the feats of the strong man, and the sight of a real fire-breathing dragon that the Great Baron himself captured!"

From behind him, Flynn heard the artificial roar. He turned and saw Big Nose and Ulf riding atop the dragon wagon with Hook Foot. The cage shook and rattled with the help of a few workers inside.

"Stress that things are free," the Baron had said.

"Join us for this special *free* show!" Andy shouted.

"People love free things, and in this case, free means they'll be so distracted and clamoring to watch, they won't notice when one of our carts peels off." The Baron had looked at Flynn and Lance. *"That's where you two come in. Just before sunset, four guards will be headed to the Antiquities Shoppe to watch the reward for the next shift."* His eyes narrowed. *"You will make sure they don't get there."*

Flynn heard a loud chime followed by four gongs. He looked up. The sun was low.

"There they are," Sideburns said, motioning to four guards who were marching across the square.

The Antiquities Shoppe was straight ahead. There was a roped-off area with a line of people waiting out front behind a sign.

VIEW THE REWARD FOR THE LOST PRINCESS HERE!

Mothers, fathers, the elderly, and the young were patiently waiting for a chance to see what the king and queen were offering as a reward. Two guards were standing outside the shoppe as patrons were allowed in and out.

"Don't worry about the guards in front of the shoppe," the Baron had assured them. *"They're not allowed to leave their post for the hour they're on duty, so chances are good they won't step inside the shoppe or see what's going on behind it."*

"Chances are good?" Big Nose had repeated nervously.

The Baron just smiled. *"Well, nothing in a heist is guaranteed, is it?"*

Flynn watched as four guards came through the front door, addressed the ones at the entrance, and moved in formation back to the castle.

"You will take your wagon around the back of the shoppe," the Baron had continued. *"There is a courtyard behind there that is completely hidden. With all the noise from the Hook brothers' performance, the acrobatics at the circus, and our fireworks, no one will hear the commotion."*

Their wagon passed the Antiquities Shoppe and rounded the corner. Just as the Baron had confirmed, there was a courtyard shrouded by trees and a tall castle wall. Who he had paid off to get that information, Flynn didn't know. He could feel his hands growing clammy as he heard fireworks set off. Behind the shoppe were empty crates and a small table with jugs of water, but it was otherwise deserted, which was both good and bad.

Good: No one else would see him betray the crew.

Bad: He'd have no backup when he tried to escape. Was there too much to take on foot? Could he steal the royal wagon and get everything inside by himself? It seemed unlikely. How would he keep the reward safe?

"This is when you will spring into action, turning the cart from a circus

wagon to a royal one that will allow you to exit the alleyway when you're done, with no one the wiser," the Baron had advised.

As soon as Sideburns came to a stop, all four boys hopped off the wagon and began cutting the knots that tied the tarp over the carriage. Once free, they stuffed it inside the wagon, where several trunks were waiting to be filled with the reward. Sideburns and Patchy effortlessly lifted out the trunks and carried them to the back door while Flynn stood guard with Lance. His best friend still wouldn't make eye contact. Instead, he scratched his eyebrow again. That had to be a sign he was nervous, and if Lance was nervous, maybe that meant he wasn't entirely on board with what was about to happen either. Flynn had to hope that was true.

"Vlad and Atilla, dressed as royal guards, will approach the line and explain that there will be a short break before anyone else can view the treasure," the Baron continued. *"To keep people happy and avoid complaints, they'll give them tickets to see a circus show on the other side of the square. Ulf will be there to perform a mime routine that includes him pretending to walk a high wire — while trying to avoid being eaten by a dragon."*

Flynn could just imagine Vlad and Atilla in front of the shoppe trying to convince people to get out of the line. They weren't the warmest and fuzziest of men. Pulling off that trick would be huge.

"Thanks to my 'conversation' with the royal sign maker, we will place this in front of the shoppe to keep anyone else from trying to walk up and see the reward." The Baron held up a new sign: *Exhibit for the rewards for our lost princess temporarily closed! Please come back this evening!*

The Baron went on. *"Next, Vlad will make the call."*

"Caw-caw!"

An impressive imitation of a birdcall — high-pitched yet distinct — filled the air, reaching them in the alley.

"That's Vlad's cue." Sideburns started to move. "He and Atilla must have already replaced the guards in front of the shoppe." He grabbed a long club from the carriage and tapped it in his calloused hands as he turned with laser focus toward the alleyway.

"Once Vlad makes the call, you should be prepared for the next shift of guards to come round the corner at any second," the Baron had said. *"So be ready."*

As if summoned, Flynn heard the sound of marching men coming closer. He made his way behind Sideburns. He could feel Lance watching him, but Flynn wasn't a fool. He couldn't blow his cover yet. If he wanted in that shoppe, he had to follow through with this part of the plan.

Sorry about this, he thought as he donned the black mask he'd tucked in his pocket.

The guards rounded the corner, and in a blink of an eye, Sideburns took a quick swing of the bat, leaving Patchy to take care of the other two. A jab to the face each and a knock on the back, and they were out cold. Patchy and Sideburns quickly pulled them into the underbrush behind the shoppe, concealing their bodies from view as he and Lance took off the men's armor and jackets, then tied their hands and legs. He and Lance each shrugged into a uniform.

"The Stabbington brothers will place the chests inside the back of the store. Then they'll come back outside and stand watch as our newest recruits fill the trunks with the reward of our dreams." He'd looked at Flynn and Lance pointedly. *"Don't mess this part up."*

Flynn watched as Sideburns pulled something small out of his pocket. Flynn recognized it immediately — the key he and Lance had retrieved from the Weasel. Sideburns slipped the key into the back door and turned the latch. The door popped open, and Sideburns slipped inside.

Flynn's heart was beating so loud, he feared everyone would hear it. He tried to calm his nerves.

Sideburns was out seconds later. "Coast is clear," he said gruffly. "Let's get these trunks in."

Sideburns and Patchy lifted the trunks and carried them into the shoppe while Flynn waited outside with Lance.

It was a strange feeling knowing he was about to go into that shoppe and fight for something entirely different than his best friend. The thought made him feel itchy, as if he hadn't bathed in days. How was he going to go against Lance, his only family?

"You're up, Rider and Strongbow," Sideburns growled. He held the door open, but Patchy blocked their way. "Patchy says if you mess this up, there will be nothing left of either of you to ship back to that orphanage. You hear me?"

Flynn winked at him. "Comforting, as always, Sideburns." He grabbed his satchel, slung it over his shoulder, and headed to the door.

That's when Patchy grabbed him by the shoulder strap and yanked him backward.

EIGHTEEN

"IT'S JUST YOU AND ME TO THE RIVER'S EDGE."
—FLYNNIGAN RIDER IN *FLYNNIGAN RIDER AND THE RIDE TO THE RIVER'S EDGE*

F lynn gagged as the strap yanked on his neck. He quickly pulled his satchel strap out of Patchy's hands. Lance stood very still and watched them.

"Patchy wants to know what you need that old bag for?" Sideburns asked.

"Weapons, of course," Flynn said. "Slingshot, mask, dog bone, harmonica, my dirty socks. Want me to open it up and let you catch a whiff?" He thought he caught Lance smirk.

Patchy let go of him, and he and Lance slipped through the door. Flynn breathed a sigh of relief.

"Once you're inside, you've got fifteen minutes to get the job done," the Baron had told them.

"I thought we had an hour," Vlad said.

The Baron's face was grim. *"We've got an hour before the next shift shows up. You boys better be long gone by then."*

"What about you?" Andy asked. *"How are you going to get out of the kingdom unseen?"*

"*I don't have to be unseen,*" the Baron reminded him. "*I've been busy playing ringmaster, remember? I haven't stolen a thing.*"

The statement reminded Flynn of something the Baron had said to him and Lance the morning they went to find the key. If you get caught, don't say you know me because I won't say I know you. The Baron had always been out for himself. Well, Flynn was going to take a page from his book now. He was alone, but he could still stop him.

Flynn heard the door lock behind him. He and Lance looked at each other. They were alone again. Wordlessly, they spread out around the shoppe.

The shoppe wasn't big. Or maybe it just looked that way because it was crammed with antiques — lamps, books, dresses, jewels, furniture piled on top of each other — all tagged with yellow slips of paper that noted the prices. There was a suit of armor that had seen better days, some sort of spear, not to mention the ugliest lamp Flynn had ever seen and a rug that was the color of pea soup. Mirrors hung on the walls, each with a varying degree of dust layered over the glass, and a jewelry counter with rings and other baubles sat on display. Flynn walked a few feet farther and spotted the velvet rope. He hurried toward it and Lance followed. As they rounded two tables stacked on top of each other, one missing a leg, he stopped short.

Behind the purple rope, there was a banner that read *Our Beloved Princess*. Beneath it was a banquet-length table with a mountain of gifts that Flynn thought only existed in dreams. There were goblets — tall, short, fat, thin, jeweled, engraved — in a variety of precious metals, and golden rattles, frames, vases, and gold plates. He spotted crowns and tiaras meant for infants and adults alike, and several priceless paintings from the Seven Kingdoms depicting the lost princess with the king and queen as a babe. (One was rather abstract and strange, so he wasn't sure how it was considered a "reward," but to each his own.) In the center of the table was a bowl of gold ostrich eggs. Flynn's eyes widened at the sight of them. Just one egg could set up Miss Clare's Home for Boys for a year.

In front of the table, people had left a memorial with flowers and candles along with notes. Lance picked up a letter and read the scratchy, childlike handwriting. "Princess, we will never stop searching till we bring you home!"

Home. Just the word formed a lump in his throat. Lance was his home. No, *Arnie* was. And now they weren't even on the same team. How had they gotten to this awful place? Since the very beginning, it had always been Eugene and Arnie plotting adventures and thinking of how they'd conquer the world. Flynn and Lance, however, were at a major crossroads.

They each moved toward the treasure at the same time.

"Flynn," Lance started to say, but Flynn cut him off.

"Me first!" Flynn said hurriedly. "Don't do this, Lance! It's my fault we're in this mess. I screwed up all of our plans—I made you join the circus and told you it was so we could start a new life, which it was, but I didn't tell you about Vedis, which was wrong. I didn't want you to think I was trying to abandon you. I just had to know what happened to my parents, Lance. I had to. And he was the first person I met who might have a clue." Lance looked away. "I never meant to hurt you or make you think you aren't my family, because you *are*. I meant what I said about my parents—if we ever find them, I wouldn't go with them if you couldn't come, too." Flynn looked down at his boots and swallowed hard. "But it doesn't matter what my dreams for us were. The truth is, my parents are gone. The whole Dark Kingdom is."

Lance looked at him. "What do you mean gone? You mean Vedis knows them? You found them?" He actually sounded excited.

"Not exactly." Flynn swallowed hard. "Vedis said anyone who lived in the Dark Kingdom was either lost or disappeared. The kingdom isn't even on the map now, which means — "

"Maybe your parents escaped," Lance interrupted now. "Maybe they are still out there somewhere looking for you." They looked at each other. "Just because Vedis said this Dark . . . Kingdom, did you call it? . . . is destroyed doesn't mean your parents are, too."

Flynn felt bolstered by hope. If Lance thought the same thing he did, then . . .

There was a pounding on the back door.

"Let's go!" Sideburns barked.

"Flynn," Lance said and stepped toward the treasure.

Flynn dove in front of him. "Wait! I can't let you do this, Lance."

Lance looked at him. "I'm not."

"I'm serious, you can't — wait, what?" Flynn floundered.

Lance smirked. "I've been trying to ask you if you had a plan, but you keep interrupting with apologies, which can be made later!" There was a pounding on the door again. "Now, are we getting this stuff out of here and to safety or what?"

Flynn reached over and bear-hugged his best friend.

"Flynn!" Lance gasped. "When was the last time you bathed?"

"Sorry." Flynn let go, but he was still grinning. "Yesterday, but I've been so nervous about you and this and the Baron that I can't stop sweating. I'm glad to have you back, Arnie."

Lance gave him a look. "You still have some groveling to do. And you owe me an apology." They both moved to the reward table and started grabbing things.

"Oh, I know. Major groveling. But first, to answer your question, I don't have an actual plan other than to say my plan is to make sure the Baron doesn't get his hands on the princess's reward. We have to keep it safe." Flynn held up a gold ostrich egg. The thing weighed a ton. He could only imagine how much it was worth.

Lance thought for a moment, then dumped a few jewels in Flynn's arms. "I've got an idea. Stay here." He jogged to the back of the shoppe and dragged both trunks forward with his own two hands.

Flynn couldn't help but look confused. "What are you doing?"

"You trust me?" Lance asked.

Flynn didn't hesitate. "It's just you and me to the River's Edge," which was a line from one of his Flynn Rider books. Lance's smile faded. "I just made it cheesy, didn't I?"

"Very cheesy," Lance agreed. He opened one of the trunks. "But that's okay. Now start loading and listen very closely to what I have to say."

Ten minutes later, Flynn knocked on the back door of the shoppe, and Sideburns opened the door with the key.

"Took you long enough!" he growled. "We're almost out of time!"

"Sorry. A lot to load. Baron will be pleased," Flynn said. "Can you help us get the second chest out of the shoppe and into the carriage?"

Sideburns looked at him. "That's your job. We have to stay here and watch for any sign of trouble." Patchy was standing in the background, holding a sword.

"From us?" Flynn acted offended. "We're trying to move as fast as we can. We've got this trunk, and it will take us a few minutes to get back and grab the second one, but if you want this whole thing to take longer . . ."

Sideburns sighed. "Why the Baron thinks you two are so great, I'll never know. Patchy, drop the sword. We have to go do their job for them." He looked at Lance as he brushed past him. "Keep an eye out for trouble."

"Any trouble and we will certainly report it," Lance told him solemnly.

The minute Sideburns and Patchy were in the shoppe, Flynn and Lance looked at each other and shut the door behind them. Lance moved a barrel of water in front of the door. Then they picked up the trunk and moved as fast as their legs would take them across the courtyard. They heaved it into the back of the carriage, then ran around to the front and climbed up. They could hear the Stabbies hollering and pounding on the door, but they ignored them.

"You know how to drive this thing?" Lance asked.

"Nope." Flynn gave the reins a crack. Nothing happened. "Hopefully I'll learn fast."

"Rider!"

Sideburns and Patchy broke open the door, knocking over the water barrel. They took one look at Flynn and Lance and started running.

"Oh boy." Flynn cracked the reins again. The horses still didn't move.

Lance grabbed the leather straps from him. "Let me try!" He gave the horses a whistle, and they zipped around the corner and out of sight, hearing the Stabbingtons shout after them.

NINETEEN

"I HOPE YOU'RE READY, BECAUSE THINGS
ARE ABOUT TO GET MESSY."

—FLYNNIGAN RIDER IN *FLYNNIGAN RIDER AND THE RIDE TO THE RIVER'S EDGE*

"How long do we think we have?" Lance snapped the reins, and the horses headed down the cobblestone street back the way they'd come.

Flynn kept looking back, waiting for the Stabbingtons to round the corner, but they couldn't give themselves away either. "We have their ride. Plus, the circus performance should be just finishing up, which means if we timed this right, we can ride straight past the Baron and make it look like it's all still part of the plan."

"Yeah, still part of the plan," Lance said as his brow started to perspire. "And the streets are pretty crowded. It's not like the Baron can come after us here, can he?"

"No! Not when all these people are around. *Oh.*" Flynn motioned to the road ahead, where the circus was supposed to be entering its final act (something about geese on horses with Hook Hand playing a melody).

Instead, the crowd was starting to disperse. Flynn could see some of the circus wagons pulling down their tarps to get ready to head out.

"Okay. Uh, Sideburns might have been right. We might have taken too long inside the shoppe."

Lance threw his head back and groaned. *"We'regoingtogetcaught we'regoingtogetcaughtwe'regoingtogetcaught."*

Flynn patted his hand as much for Lance's benefit as for his own. "No, we're still fine. The wagon is supposed to be coming through right now, remember? We just need to act natural." He placed his hands on his lap, crossed his arms, then crossed his right leg over the left, switched positions, and put his left leg over the right. "Stay calm. As long as the Baron isn't around, we don't have anything to worry about."

"Flynn," Lance squeaked. "The Baron is *right there.*"

A cart selling lanterns moved out of the way, and Flynn saw the Baron standing a few yards off, directing two wagons out of the village. That part of the plan had been carefully timed so that the wagons would disappear over the bridge, while all of the kingdom focused on the lanterns lifting into the sky above.

"Just keep going." Flynn attempted to smile and speak out of the side of his mouth at the same time.

"What if he stops us?"

"He won't."

"Flynn! What if he does?"

Flynn kept smiling at the Baron, who was standing on the busy village street in his ringmaster jacket, an aging velvet coat too warm for the weather. He saw Flynn and Lance and waved them over.

"Now what?" Lance hissed.

"Uh . . . pull over and don't reveal anything other than that we're headed to the rendezvous point. And don't bring up Sideburns or Patchy! If he asks, we'll say they're in the back."

"Got it." Lance wiped his brow with a handkerchief.

"Thank you for stopping, gentlemen!" the Baron boomed.

It took Flynn a moment to realize why he was calling them gentlemen or being so official — they were still dressed as royal guards in a royal carriage. They needed a reason to speak to one another. "Good afternoon!"

"Could you tell me if the viewing of the reward for the lost princess has resumed at the . . . oh, what did the villagers say it was called? The Antiquities Shoppe?"

"That has finished for the day, sir. I'm sorry," Lance replied. "I believe the lanterns are launching soon."

The Baron nodded and leaned in closer as men and women with children walked by them, carrying lanterns. "So . . . it's done?"

Flynn spoke calmly. "Yep! We got exactly what we came for."

The Baron's smile widened. "Good! See you at the — "

"STOP!" a voice interrupted. "Stop them!"

Flynn turned around. Several guards were barreling toward them on horseback. People everywhere turned to look. At the same time, Flynn saw Patchy and Sideburns — back in their street clothes, running alongside the guards.

"That's them!" Sideburns yelled. "Those are the men who stole the princess's treasure!"

Flynn and the Baron slowly looked at each other. It didn't take the Baron more than a second to put two and two together. His face began to redden. Flynn didn't wait. He nudged Lance. "GO!"

Lance cracked the reins, and the carriage took off at top speed. People in the village dove out of the way as the carriage careened down the street, headed straight toward the bridge.

"What do we do?" Lance cried. "We can't outrun them!"

Flynn thought quickly. Up ahead, several royal carriages were going way too slowly for his liking. "Lance! What about Wa-Gone?"

Lance's eyes widened with recognition. "Yes, the ole wagon switcheroo! From *The Secret of Calypso Cove* book! Let's give them something to scratch their helmets over!" He gave the reins another crack — he was getting really good at this driving thing — and the carriage moved faster, falling in line with two other carriages, making it harder to see who was who. They were quickly approaching the bridge out of the kingdom, which was their chance to make a getaway.

"Flynn . . ." Lance sounded nervous. "What if they recognize us? They'll never let us over the bridge."

"Um . . . I didn't think of that." Flynn thought fast. "Maybe we don't use the bridge to leave."

"This wagon doesn't float!" Lance cried. "We need that bridge to get out of town."

"Thinking!" Flynn cried as the guards approached. "Okay, they'll probably follow the carriage that goes out of town, right? Thinking we're racing away?"

"Which is what we're doing!"

Flynn looked at the crossroads by the bridge up ahead. "So if we stay on the island and blend in, they won't look for us, right?"

Lance looked pensive. "It's worth a shot." He pulled up to the guards.

Flynn gave them a wave. "Nice day for a ride, isn't it?" Three different streets, including the bridge out of town, were straight ahead of them.

"Uh, yes," said the first guard. "Where are you headed?"

"To meet the captain," Flynn said quickly. "The lantern thing for the lost princess."

The guard nodded as if he'd said the right thing. "Take a left up ahead."

Lance took a hard left and barreled down a bumpy residential street headed directly for the water. Flynn turned around. The other two carriages kept going straight. Flynn breathed a sigh of relief.

"See anyone behind us?" Lance asked.

The sky was now a pinkish purple and the light was starting to dim, but there was no sign of trouble. "Nope! It worked! We lost them!"

"Good!" Lance smacked his arm.

"OWW!" Flynn held his arm. "What was that for?"

"I'm still mad at you," Lance said.

"I know." Flynn rubbed his shoulder.

"If you'd come clean sooner, we could have avoided fighting and gotten away from the circus before any of this even happened!" Lance pulled over. "We have to ditch this carriage." He stopped the horses and immediately started climbing down.

"I wanted to, but there was never a good time." Flynn jumped out behind him. They went to the back of the carriage, lifted the tarp at the same time, and began tugging on the heavy trunk. "Quick! Help me with the chest."

"Where are we taking this thing?" Lance said. "And you could have found a good time at some point — we were at the circus almost two weeks!"

Flynn looked around for a hiding spot. "I know. But you were always with Atilla."

"Because I like to cook," Lance said, looking around as they placed the trunk on the ground. "And the kitchen crew made me feel like I was at home — after you had torn our home out from under us." Lance's eyes widened. "Ooh! What about a boat for one of the lantern launches!"

Flynn clutched his heart. "Yes! And the other thing — *harsh*. You know it was time to go." They lifted the trunk again and walked quickly to the river.

"I know, but we always said we'd leave the home on our own terms . . . Could you have added anything more to this thing?" Lance groaned as he tried to keep the trunk steady so it didn't topple.

"Couldn't . . . leave . . . anything . . . behind." Flynn tried to talk under the mounting weight. "And we did leave on our own terms." Lance looked at him. "Okay, *my* terms. I should have been straight with you."

The sound of shouting, hooves, and wagons racing across bumpy cobblestone streets was growing closer.

"Darn straight you should have!" Lance accidentally rammed a family with the chest as they neared the water. "Sorry! Coming through!" He practically swung the trunk onto the boat.

"Hey! That's our boat," a man said as Lance jumped into it and pulled the trunk in farther. Flynn shoved past and jumped in himself.

"Sorry!" Flynn said to him. "We really need it."

"He has a lot of apologizing to do," Lance said to the man as Flynn pushed them off with an oar just as Sideburns appeared.

"Rider! Strongbow!" Sideburns shouted as he ran down the street.

Folks began to notice the commotion, but the boat was already drifting away.

"Uh-oh. We've got more company." Lance tried to row faster. "It's our crew."

Patchy, Sideburns, Hook Foot, Big Nose, Andy, and Vlad were racing down the sloped street. Even the guys they'd just started to call friends looked ready to tear them limb from limb.

"I don't think we're their crew anymore," Flynn said with a gulp.

"That's okay. Maybe someday they'll understand—we couldn't steal from a lost princess." Lance smiled at Flynn.

"Exactly," Flynn agreed. "I'm really sorry for everything."

"You better be," Lance said. "From here on out, we are honest with each other."

"Always. Promise. Cross my heart and hope to die."

"Can we not talk about dying right now? The other guys are getting into boats!"

The rest of the crew had stolen boats and were making their way into the water, shouting, and paddling as fast as they could, the Stabbington brothers leading the way.

"That's okay," Flynn thought, looking across the lake, where he saw a light blinking in the distance. "The rendezvous point is up ahead."

"I hope you're right about this next part," Lance squeaked as he dumped a bucket of water overboard. Somehow they were starting to take on water.

Flynn looked at Lance. "Do you trust me?"

"Hey, that's my line!"

"Well, do you?" Flynn asked.

"Yes," Lance groaned. "Despite everything, yes!"

"Then keep paddling." Flynn kept his eye on the light at the shoreline.

When you get the treasure onto the carriage and make your way across the bridge, a flashing lantern will tell you which way to go," the Baron had told them. *"There will be a change of clothes and some horses waiting to take you on to Vardaros, where we will all reunite."*

Flynn looked back at the kingdom for what he suspected would be the last time. The reflection on the water was beautiful. All around them, boats were lit up with lanterns coming alive, their flames igniting one by one till it looked like there were a thousand fireflies descending on the kingdom at the same time. It was a beautiful way to remember the lost princess. *If she could only see this and know how much the kingdom misses her,* Flynn thought.

"I can't even tell who is who anymore." Lance interrupted his thoughts. "All the boats look the same. Do you see the crew anywhere? The Stabbingtons? The Baron? Where are the guards?"

Flynn squinted into the darkness. He really wished he had grabbed a lantern himself. "Maybe we lost them for now. Let's keep going."

It took them a while to get across the water, but they tried to keep the boat steady, Lance on lookout and Flynn trying to steer the boat toward the blinking light. Finally, their boat drifted toward land. From where Flynn sat, he could see the lantern sitting alone on the rocky shoreline. There was no sign of anyone still being there.

"Flynn, I don't know about this."

"Trust me." Flynn jumped from the front of the small boat and began to pull it ashore with Lance and the chest still inside. "We have the Baron *beat*." The last word fell out of him as he was yanked by the back of his shirt and his whole body was swung into the air.

"Where do you think you're going with our reward?" Sideburns growled.

Several men appeared through the trees and converged on the boat at the same time, grabbing Lance and the chest of treasure and pulling them from the boat. Vlad held Lance up by the back of his guard uniform and marched over to stand alongside Sideburns, who still had Flynn.

Hook Hand pried open the chest and swung a lantern over the contents. The box glittered with gold. "It's all here, Baron! They gave us the junk and were trying to make off with our reward!" He held up a lamp with a base that was peeling off.

"I'll have you know the Antiquities Shoppe considers that stuff valuable." Flynn gulped as Sideburns held him higher. "Okay, so maybe it's not as fine as the actual treasure, but it's kind of nice-looking."

"This is nice-looking?" Hook Hand reached into the other trunk of junk and grabbed a lamp. The base fell off the lamp, leaving Hook Hand with just the top shade.

"Maybe it was on sale," Flynn said, his voice squeaking.

"I can't believe you two! Traitors! You thought a change of clothes and a new wagon were waiting so you could escape here with our loot," Hook Foot sneered. He held his hook foot up in the air to take a swing at them, and several of the other crew members egged him on. Staylan stood on the sidelines, giving Flynn the dirtiest of looks.

"You have this all wrong! I can explain!" Flynn tried to keep his face away from Hook Foot's blade.

"Could you?" asked the Baron, emerging from the darkness. "I would love an explanation, Rider, as to why two of my finest new recruits would double-cross me. Because right now I want to drown the two of you in the river." Some of the crew cheered.

"Double-cross? No!" Flynn said, attempting a laugh. "We were holding the real treasure for safekeeping!"

"Oh yeah? When were you going to give it back?" Vlad asked.

"Now, of course, which is why we're here," Lance jumped in. "We knew there would be heat on us when the guards woke up, so we took the real treasure and got out of there, leaving the Stabbies with a box of junk to keep the guards off our scent. If they caught them, they'd let the boys off while we made off with the real goods."

The Baron looked at them, saying nothing at first. "That wasn't part of the plan."

"No, no it wasn't," Flynn said, "but plans change, am I right?"

"So it wasn't cold feet?" the Baron growled. "You didn't grow a conscience and decide you couldn't take the princess's treasure?"

Flynn opened up his mouth to lie, but he couldn't do it. He was exhausted from all the lies and the trickery. He glanced at Lance apologetically. "Okay, I did feel bad — it's her reward money!" The other men groaned. "You're the Baron! You can nab any treasure you want! I just saw it and thought, why do you need this?"

"Flynn," Lance moaned.

The Baron paused for a moment. "Because I can have it. It was there for the taking, and I put in weeks and months of planning to get it." His face started to redden, and he formed a fist. "Months! And you two messed it up! Don't you think the guards are going to wonder who you work for?" Flynn looked down. "We could end up in the gallows. Is that what you want?"

"I think he does!" someone called out.

"We did get you something," Lance said. "Take a look at the chest. Right on top of your junk that we found there is a jade necklace."

"It matched the bracelet I scored you last week," Flynn said.

One of the men went back to the chest the Baron had in his possession and fished out the necklace. He handed it to the Baron, who held it up in the moonlight.

In the distance, Flynn heard yelling. He could see the bridge to the isle, and it was filled with guards and horses heading their way.

"Baron? We don't have much time," Vlad said. "What do you want me to do with them? Want me to bind them and toss them in the river?"

Flynn gulped. "That seems extreme. Wouldn't you be happier doing something more revengelike?" He looked at Lance. "Like, I don't know, sending us back in the boat with the bogus chest of treasure while you all drive away?" Flynn's eyes went wide.

"FLYNN!" Lance threw his head back and groaned. "Why are you giving them ideas?"

The Baron tucked the jade necklace into his jacket pocket and snapped his fingers. "Do it," he told Atilla. "Bind their hands, gag them, and ship them off. Everyone else to the wagons. Load the reward in mine. We'll take our chances and try to get away. We certainly won't be coming back to this kingdom."

Vlad looked crestfallen. "I really can't toss them in the water?"

"No!" the Baron roared as the shouting drew closer. "Do what I said! They'll take the fall for the break-in, and we'll get away with the real treasure. By the time they realize the switch, we'll be in Vardaros. Good luck finding us there." Some of the crew laughed.

The others rushed him and Lance back into the boat and threw their trunk of junk in with them. Atilla gagged them.

"Andy, tie them up!" Atilla barked. "And don't either of you move."

Andy looked miserable as he boarded the boat and tied Lance's hands, then Flynn's. "I'm sorry about this," he whispered. He tied the rope around Flynn's wrists and looked at it. "I'm going to leave a gap," he whispered. "Maybe you can get away before the guards get you. Good luck, guys." He jumped off the boat, then followed the others to the wagons.

Atilla shoved them off into the water again. "Good luck, fellas! It isn't personal, you know," he said to Lance. "You're a good cook. It's just, out here, it's every person for themself, as the Baron says." He ran to the nearest wagon.

The Baron gave them one last look. "You're lucky I didn't do far worse to you two. If it wasn't for this necklace and the fact I now have the treasure, well . . . next time I won't be so kind. Do not cross my path again." He cracked the reins and peeled off into the night.

Flynn watched the lanterns cast a warm glow over the water as their boat began to drift. The rest of the boats were already retreating by the time he worked the knot off his wrist. He took off his gag and went for Lance's.

"Finally!" he groaned. "Did you check the chest?"

Flynn opened the chest and saw the bad lamp and a bunch of rusted cufflinks and busted picture frames lying on top. "Yep! This is the one!" He reached his hand in and pulled out a beautiful gold ostrich egg. "I can't believe they didn't think to dig *through* the chest before deeming this junk."

Lance pulled out a gold cuff bracelet. "That's the Stabbington brothers for you! How far do you think the Baron will get before he figures out we switched chests on purpose and he had the real treasure the whole time?"

Flynn grinned. "Hopefully not till he gets to Vardaros." Flynn looked to the shoreline. "Because we still have work to do."

Lance sighed as he looked at the bracelet from all angles. "Seems a shame to return all this stuff to a lost princess when Miss Clare could really benefit from it."

"*Lance* . . ." Flynn warned.

"I know. I know. We'll figure out another way to help the orphanage. Let's get to land and return the treasure."

TWENTY

"YOU KNOW THE GREAT THING ABOUT BEGINNINGS? THEY'RE
THE BEGINNING! IT MEANS WE'RE ONLY GETTING STARTED."

—FLYNNIGAN RIDER IN *FLYNNIGAN RIDER AND THE HUNT FOR THE RED PEARL*

"I can't believe we're breaking back into the Antiquities Shoppe," Lance said as they huddled around the back door and tried to use a pin to break the lock. Things would be so much easier if they still had the key. "Déjà vu."

"Except this time, we're breaking in for the right reasons." Flynn fiddled with the keyhole for another few seconds before hearing the click. "Got it! We're in!" He pushed the door open. The shoppe was completely dark.

Everything in the kingdom was closed, the festival having ended after the lantern display. They had carried the reward in sacks they plucked from an unoccupied street cart while workers cleaned up confetti and trash from the street. The guards, it seemed, had taken to the mainland to search for the ruffians who had stolen the princess's reward. The only sound was a man whistling as he swept. He and Lance had moved quickly, not breathing till they were in the shoppe's alleyway, and now they were actually inside. All was going according to their new, on-the-fly plan. Maybe *he* had a knack for heists. The noble kind.

"Five minutes and we are out of here," Flynn whispered. "Just be careful not to — " He heard the crash and turned around.

Lance held a broken vase. "Sorry! It's hard moving around in the dark."

"A few more steps," Flynn said, "then we'll put the reward back on the table and no one will even know we were here." The floor creaked as he took another step.

Suddenly the shoppe flooded with light. The captain of the guard and six men with swords stared angrily back at them.

"Want to bet on that?" the captain of the guard said. "Guards! Cuff them!"

"So this is what the castle looks like," Flynn marveled as they were marched across a marble foyer with high ceilings and beautiful archways, with their arms tied behind their backs. The massive hallway, lined with rugs like he'd seen in the Baron's tent, had portraits of royals on the walls. If they could get a few wagons inside that space, there would be some epic races. "This place is much bigger than it looks on the outside."

"I'm loving all the art and sculptures," Lance agreed. "Ooh! Can you imagine what kind of kitchen they have?"

"Quiet!" the captain of the guard barked. "This isn't a tour! We had to wake the king and queen up to see you two. They wanted a word as soon as they heard about their daughter's reward." He steered Flynn and Lance into a large room.

Flynn was actually pretty nervous. They'd stolen their daughter's treasure and been caught by the captain, who had also seen them run from the Snuggly Duckling a few weeks back. "We'd gotten word that there was a group of traveling bandits working their way through the kingdom," the captain had said when he cuffed them. "Guess we found them."

Of course, it was the Baron he was after, but turning in his old boss when the circus caravan was halfway to Vardaros seemed like a foolish move. Lance and he agreed — the Baron could have disposed of them right there on the riverbed, but he hadn't. Who knew — their paths might cross again. Why dig a bigger hole for themselves? Besides, if there was one thing the crew had taught him in the past two weeks — aside from all the elaborate tricks and thieving maneuvers — it was that ruffians didn't rat out other ruffians.

"Presenting the king and queen — *yawn* — " announced one of the members of the royal court.

The guards in the room stood up straighter, their chins all perfectly in line as the king and queen, wearing robes, were ushered through a side door with a large wooden sunburst etched into it. At the sight of them, Flynn and Lance dropped to one knee and bowed their heads. These were the royals they'd only seen in portraits and during one procession through the village when they'd seen half of the king's left arm. But here they were, standing right in front of them, and wow, did the king look angry.

"These are the boys who took my daughter's reward?" His voice echoed in the large room. "You're lucky I don't have you sent straight to the dungeons and held there for years!" His blue eyes were dark, and his mustache and beard looked unkempt, since he'd been woken to come see them. Which meant he was extra cranky.

"Dear," a softer voice spoke. Flynn looked up to see the queen put a hand on her husband's shoulder. She had long dark brown hair and large green eyes. Flynn knew at once where he'd seen eyes just like them — the lost princess's mural in the village. The baby looked just like her mother. "Let them speak. Maybe they can explain."

"Explain? They stole our daughter's reward!"

"Dear," she said again, more pointedly. She looked at Flynn encouragingly. "They must have had a good reason."

Flynn and Lance looked at each other. Lance was sweating again, the beads dripping down his forehead. If there was any time to use Flynn's gift of gab, it was now.

"Your Highnesses, we didn't mean for this to happen," Flynn said, and the king made a noise. "When the guards found us, we were returning the reward to the shoppe."

The king snorted. "Returning? Well, that's rich."

"It's the truth." Flynn tried being serious for a change. "We were supposed to steal it for someone, but we had a change of heart and grabbed it to protect it from the thieves."

"What thieves?" the king asked.

"I believe his name was the Weasel?" Lance said, thinking fast. "But he's long gone."

"He thinks he has the treasure, but what he really has is a chest full of worthless junk from the Antiquities Shoppe," Flynn added. "It's just a few broken lamps and strange-looking sculptures. We're sorry to have taken that stuff, but we had to make him think he had the real treasure."

"So you stole the reward to *protect* the reward?" the queen asked, looking confused.

Flynn shrugged. "Yes. It was the only way."

"But why?" the queen pressed. "If you'd gotten away with the real treasure, why not take it and run?"

"Because it—well, it wasn't the right thing to do," Lance said. "Those treasures were meant for the princess, and if they can be used to help someone find her, then that's what it should be used for."

Flynn thought of his own parents. "We know keeping families

together is important. Lance here has been mine ever since we were little. There is nothing I wouldn't do for him." Flynn smiled at his best friend. "Just like I know there is nothing you wouldn't do for your daughter. The treasure should stay here till someone can claim it for finding the princess."

"The princess is lucky to have you both, and we hope you find her someday," Lance added. "That's why we returned the treasure. We wouldn't have felt right taking away your hope."

The queen whispered something in the king's ear. The king nodded. Flynn noticed his eyes looked a bit misty. The queen turned back to the boys and smiled. "Guards, you can uncuff them."

"What? But, Your Highness!" the captain started.

"Unhand them," she repeated. "They are free to leave."

Flynn and Lance looked at each other, stunned. "Thank you, Your Highness."

The queen looked at him. "Next time, if you find yourself in trouble, think about doing anything *other* than stealing to help solve the situation." She gave them a small smile. "I'm not sure every kingdom is as forgiving."

Flynn and Lance bowed. Flynn felt one of the guard's hands on his shoulder, but he pulled out of his grasp, remembering something else he still needed to do. "If I may, there's one more thing we were hoping you could help us with."

"Oh?" The king raised an eyebrow. "Is there something other than your freedom you want?"

Flynn's face began to burn. Lance looked at him strangely. "Uh, yes, but it's not for us, actually . . . it's, um . . ."

Realization flickered on Lance's face. "It's for Miss Clare's Home for Boys. We, uh, used to be residents."

"Yes, used to be," Flynn said hastily. "We've aged out, but Miss Clare who runs the home is wonderful, and fully competent. Don't let that tax collector Kurtis Frost tell you otherwise."

"Yeah!" Lance agreed. "She's wonderful to all the boys, and we don't care what Frost says. She doesn't deserve to get her aid cut."

"Aid cut?" The queen looked baffled. "Why, we'd never cut money from an orphanage."

The king scratched his chin. "Kurtis Frost, you say? Hmm . . . I've had a few other complaints about this tax collector and people's aid not turning up. Makes me wonder if he's the one pocketing their funds. Guards?" he called to them. "Put out a warrant for Kurtis Frost's arrest. I'd like to speak to him."

Flynn and Lance grinned at each other.

Kurtis Frost would bother Miss Clare and the Home for Boys no more.

The king rose. "Well, if that's all, I'm headed back to bed. Good night, boys, and . . . good luck. I don't expect our paths to cross again."

"Oh, no, sir! Absolutely not," Flynn promised. Why would he ever have reason for an audience with the king in the future?

But before he could give it too much thought, the guards were escorting him and Lance out of the castle and unceremoniously placing them in a carriage. Fifteen minutes later, they dropped them off at the bridge out of the kingdom.

"Don't come back unless you've got something to contribute to the kingdom," the guard barked before slamming the carriage door shut and driving off.

Flynn and Lance looked at each other. The only sound in the night sky was crickets. The boys started to whoop and holler, high-fiving and hugging.

"I did not think we were getting out of there!" Lance said.

"Neither did I!" Flynn said with a laugh.

"That treasure was something though, wasn't it?" Lance said wistfully. "We could have really helped Miss Clare and the boys. I feel bad we left the home and haven't helped them the way we said we would."

Flynn grinned. "Who says we still can't help them?" He opened his satchel and pulled out the gold ostrich egg.

"WHAT? I can't believe you . . . I can't believe you . . . When did you . . . ?" Lance was flabbergasted. "You said we couldn't take anything!"

Flynn shrugged. He was pretty pleased with himself. "I don't think the king and queen will miss one little egg."

Lance's eyes widened. "This should pay the orphanage's taxes for years!"

"I hope so," said Flynn. He took another look at the egg and saw his reflection in its shiny surface. He flipped his hair to one side, then the other. Then he shook his head and put the egg back in his satchel. He'd have plenty of time to learn who he wanted to be. Right now, Flynn was just happy to have Lance by his side. He hoisted his satchel higher on his shoulder and looked at his best friend again. "And if not, we'll figure it out." Flynn thought of a line from his Flynn Rider books and smiled. "Things don't always go as planned," he said.

"No, they don't." Lance looked at the open road ahead of them. "So after we drop this egg off to Miss Clare, what do we do next?" His smile faltered slightly. "Should we try to go to the Dark Kingdom Vedis told you about?"

"Maybe," Flynn said thoughtfully. "When we know where it is, *if* we ever find out where it is, but I don't need to go on a wild goose chase to find what I already have." For once, he felt completely content. "A real family is the one you make for yourself along the way," he said, thinking of what Miss Clare always told them. "And you're mine."

"Water is thicker than blood," Lance agreed, tears welling. Flynn felt himself choke up, too. They both quickly wiped their eyes.

"So . . . if we're not looking for the Dark Kingdom, where are we headed?" Lance asked.

In the distance, the sky was starting to brighten. A new day was dawning. Flynn smiled. He put his arm around Lance. "That's the beauty of our new lives, Lance Strongbow. We can go anywhere we want."

ACKNOWLEDGMENTS

I have loved Flynn Rider from the moment I heard the opening lines of *Tangled* ("This is the story of how I died. But don't worry, this is actually a fun story and the truth is it isn't even mine."). So getting to write an origin story for Eugene Fitzherbert was both exhilarating . . . and terrifying. Thankfully, I was in the best of hands with my incredible editor Jocelyn Davies, who was more than willing to talk for hours about all things Flynn until we knew exactly how our favorite rogue would spend his days at age twelve. Then when Jocelyn was off giving birth to Disney's newest cast member, I was in equally good hands with editor Brittany Rubiano, who helped me bring this story across the finish line.

Whenever I had any questions about Flynn, I was fortunate enough to go to someone who knows Eugene/Flynn inside and out: *Tangled: The Series* co-creator Chris Sonnenburg. I'm thankful I could text him with the most random questions ("Does Flynn know the titles of any of his beloved Flynn Rider books?") and he'd have an answer. I'll never forget the day he braved the Long Island Railroad to talk to me about Flynn in person when I wasn't able to get into New York City and meet with him. Chris, you're truly a class act!

A warmest thank-you to the artistic talents of Erwin Madrid for this epic young Flynn cover and to the entire team at Disney Books (including Kieran Scott, Seale Ballenger, Lyssa Hurvitz, Dina Sherman, Cassidy Leyendecker, Sara Liebling, Guy Cunningham, David Jaffe, Meredith Jones, Marybeth Tregarthen, and Phil Buchanan) for all you've done to infuse Disney magic into this series. To Zachary Levi, whose voice lived in my head for months as I tried to nail "Flynn speak," thank you for creating a character like no other. And to *Tangled* superfan and fellow author Taylor Simonds, I'm so glad I had you on speed dial. You could easily win a *Tangled* trivia contest!

To my agent, Dan Mandel, I can't imagine being on this ride with anyone but you. Someday we will make it to WDW together, where I owe you a mountain of Mickey ice cream bars and cups of Dole Whip to thank you for all you've done for my career.

As Flynn learns on his journey, life is so much better when you have those you love to share it with. Thank you to my Disney-loving family — my husband, Mike, and two boys, Tyler and Dylan, who have gotten used to walking into the house and finding *Tangled* playing at all times day and night. This adventure would be nothing without you.